SHORT STUFF

Short Stuff

NEW ENGLISH STORIES FROM QUÉBEC

EDITED BY

Claude Lalumière

Véhicule Press

The publisher gratefully acknowledges the support of The Canada Council for the Arts for its publishing program, the Book Publishing Industry Development Program of the Department of Canadian Heritage, and the Société de développement des entreprises culturelles du Québec (SODEC).

Cover art and design: J.W. Stewart
Typesetting: Simon Garamond
Printing: AGMV/Marquis Imprimeur Inc.

LIBRARY AND ARCHIVES CANADA CATALOGUING IN PUBLICATION

Short stuff : new English stories from Quebec / edited by Claude Lalumière.

Forty stories by the winners and finalists of the CBC-QWF short story competitions, 2002-2005.
ISBN 1-55065-202-8

1. Short stories, Canadian (English)—Quebec (Province)
2. Canadian fiction (English)—21st century. I. Lalumière, Claude

PS8329.5.Q4S54 2005   C813'.01089714   C2004-906574-2

Véhicule Press
P.O.B. 125, Place du Parc Station, Montréal, Québec, Canada H2X 4A3
www.cvehiculepress.com

Distributed in Canada by LitDistCo, and in the United States by Independent Publishers Group (IPG).

Printed in Canada on ancient forest friendly paper.

Contents

2003-2004 Honourable Mentions

Deborah Ostrovsky
As Amadoras 80

Pierre W. Plante
Weathering the Storm 84

Ibi Kaslik
Bats 89

Matthew Anderson
Marathon of Hope 93

Brent Laughren
The Tin Ceiling 97

Kaarla Sundström
Widow 101

Marguerite Deslauriers
Skin 104

Neil Kroetsch
Barry, It's Alright 108

Lynn Henderson
How to Be 112

Claudia Morrison
Landings 117

Preface

A SECOND VOLUME.

That has a nice sound to it. It evokes growth. And, when you consider the number of writers whose work is gathered in this second collection, it absolutely speaks of the flourishing talent around us. Ripe for the opportunity.

And that's what the QWF / CBC Québec Short Story competition has been for the past six years. An opportunity for Québec's emerging and seasoned writers to take up the challenge and offer us their best. And for the CBC, the opportunity to discover, to develop, to showcase, and to enrich the radio experience with riveting, moving, sometimes shocking, and always original works by Québec writers.

Not just an opportunity. A privilege, really. And one that, through two anthologies so far, has been given tangible evidence by Véhicule Press. Nothing like a hard copy between your hands to make corporeal the hours of invention and hard work.

Enjoy.

Patricia Pleszczynska
Regional Director Radio and Television
CBC Québec

Foreword

WHEN I WAS ASKED to provide the foreword for this anthology celebrating the best of the CBC/QWF short fiction contest I was, of course, honoured. But that sentiment quickly gave way to incredulity. When I sat down to start writing this, all I could think about was readers scratching their head and puzzling aloud "Who the hell is Neale McDevitt?"

A fair question, to be sure, and one that gave me great pause while composing this. I guess I was asked because I am living proof of the value—the absolute necessity—of fiction competitions, this one in particular. In fact, Katherine Gombay once referred to me as "the poster boy" for this contest.

Now, those people who know me would agree that I am a potential poster boy for a great many things—fiscal irresponsibility and drunken loutishness, to name a few—but a literary competition? It seems a bit of a stretch. Until you hear my story.

In 2000 I entered this competition with "Honey-Tongued Hooker," a dark little tale about an encounter with a teenage prostitute. Being an absolute novice, completely unpublished, and entirely unknown, I worked and reworked and reworked my story until I hardly recognized it from the original. I dutifully wrote out my check to cover the entry fee, addressed a large manila envelope (I thought folding it into a regular envelope would ruin the overall presentation), lovingly slipped my pristine—and unfolded—manuscript inside, and sealed it shut with an unspoken invocation to whatever patron saint is unfortunate enough to have unknown Canadian short-story writers fall under their jurisdiction (an entry-level job among saints, I suspect).

Apparently, said saint was having a slow day or had some end-of-month quotas to fill because, lo and behold, I was named one of the three winners of the contest that year. The award ceremony was swanky (free wine; winner's check; more free wine!), and the winners were told that our stories would be adapted as short radio dramas and included in the very first anthology. Wow. It made me feel like a real writer—for a day, at least.

You can't downplay that huge moment, in which, however humbly, one finally feels like a writer. No matter how short-lived it may be, it is an accomplishment unlike any other. And although it is sometimes difficult to recreate that momentous feeling, once enjoyed, it is something you will pursue forever.

Now plenty of writers greater than me have never won, or even entered, literary contests. Indeed, mixing competition and creativity seems to bruise the delicate sensibilities of many critics, who huff that art should be above the base scrape and jostle of contests. For my part, there was something about having one of my stories judged favourably by a jury of real writers and readers that, to some extent, validated my effort. It wasn't the winning that made me feel like a writer (although that worked wonders for my ego, to be sure), it was having people take my work seriously. What more can a writer ask than to have good readers?

And lest I get too highfalutin in all this, let's not forget that contests mean deadlines and dollars. Most writers I know are either lazy layabouts like me or are perpetually in the throes of some sort of debilitating creative block. Nothing, and I mean nothing, cures either condition as quickly and miraculously as deadlines and dollars.

Winning this contest led directly to the publication of my first book, *One Day, Even Trevi Will Crumble.* One of the jurors that year, author Kenneth J. Harvey, told me that, if I was looking to get the story in print, I should contact Barry Callaghan in Toronto. Barry runs *Exile* magazine and, according to Kenneth, was a sucker for my type of writing. Kenneth also asked, in an off-handed way, if I had a manuscript kicking around, as Barry also ran Exile Editions and was always looking for new Canadian writers.

Once again, I dutifully printed out my story and wrote what may have been the most sweated-over cover letter in the history of CanLit. "Hi Barry ... CBC/QWF contest winner ... Kenneth J. Harvey ... *love* your magazine [A sugar-coated lie—I had never even read it]... P.S. I have a manuscript ... Please publish ... everything..."

A little more than a month later, the story appeared in *Exile*—my first piece of published fiction—and I was signing a book contract, albeit a modest one.

The book came out on 29 November 2002 (the same day my daughter Charlotte was born; it was a very fertile spring for me), got some good reviews, was prominently on display at Indigo—wedged between *The Polished Hoe* and *Life of Pi* (one of the few advantages of working as a stock boy at Indigo)—and, of course, sold very few copies. In November 2003, however, the book was named Best First Book of the Year by the QWF. Book sales be damned, I crowed to myself.

Based largely on the strength of my collection, I landed a generous grant from the Conseil des Arts et des Lettres du Québec. I also was named to the Writers in Cegeps program, in which I actually get paid to go and talk to college students about my writing. Yes, I said *paid*. Real money.

I have now had my work published on both sides of the border. And, because I am longer completely unknown, I suspect my dossier has been passed on to the Patron Saint of Obscure Canadian Authors. Most importantly, thanks to the many good things that have happened as a direct result of winning the contest back in 2000, I feel like a writer almost every day—and not just because I am frustrated, behind schedule, and jealous of the success of my peers. For the good stuff, too.

Neale McDevitt
Montreal, December 2004

2002-2003

JOHN BROOKE

The Death of PJ Barfard

dreaming into the crystalline leisure class
— Jon Paul Fiorentino, Resume Drowning

It was sultry, breezy, perfectly unworldly the day PJ Barfard dropped
dead on the eighteenth green. It happened immediately upon sinking
an incredible ninety-foot putt. It was coming up five, that time of
day when the sun is nearest and the cross-lit terrain shows most
smoothly. We were cooling off on the clubhouse deck, watching as
they approached—PJ Barfard, JR Briscoe, GD Smart, old PJ striding
tall and loose ... Too loose, in retrospect; his soul already separating,
the sun flowing through him—his clothes appearing to shimmer,
his unsnipped summer hair burnished by the glow. His rangy shadow
stretched across the green. Birds were beginning to gather. Now that
we think back on it.

Yes, we all agree: there were birds for the death of PJ.

You might say that we here at the club lead a privileged life.
That's a knee-jerk thing to say and patently untrue. We remain as
uninformed and vulnerable as anyone when it comes to death. Take
PJ Barfard: PJ was amazed that his putt went in. We all saw it: his
smile, half-formed. Then he was dead. If you can show us insider
privilege or a silver spoon or an old-boy network in that equation,
we'll invite you for a complimentary round.

(You must wear a collared shirt and shoes with plastic spikes.)

PJ lined it up in his usual fastidious way. He shifts around on all
fours like a ponderous bear, assessing the break from every
conceivable angle; then he stands over it with that flurry of quick
practices which have no relation at all to the actual stroke; then
another long look surveying his intended route. It takes forever. PJ

once admitted it was willful, all part of a well-honed sense of psychological brinkmanship, a golf variation on the way he played things so well so often when he was doing business. Then he putted.

Count off ninety feet. Add in a downhill slope, swerving left to right and back to left with a hump at the eight-foot mark, the pond waiting fifteen short feet beyond. It seemed PJ hit it too hard, it ran too boldly as it started on its journey. As one, we thought: Uh-oh, poor PJ, headed for a bath. If he missed, he would have surely gone off the far side and into the pond. Add four strokes—one out, one on, two down. PJ would have joined us on the deck, eyes dull with the shame of it. He would've gotten drunk and maundered on about sex with his secretary, his latest profits, his wife who ignores him, his problems with his sons. We would have indulged him, challenged him, played with him (the secretary had been twenty years ago), comforted him, and let him buy the drinks. He'd have gone home, if not happy, at least secure in his sense of belonging, ready to try again another day.

But PJ sank it, seemed surprised ... seemed verging on joy, then was dead.

As it took its leftward curve, it appeared to relax and find its proper speed. PJ's putt was looking like a putt that's bound for glory! ... until it reached the apex of the hump. Once over the hump, PJ's putt was transformed again, moving from the realm of artistry (whether intended or not has remained moot), past luck and into the world of reckless desperation. Members recognize desperation on the eighteenth green in the same way non-members might note a café or fruit store opening on the same shadowy corner of their community where a dozen predecessors have failed utterly in as many years. Our founding members (PJ was one) conferred with the man who designed the course and instructed him to build the slope on the eighteenth green just so. When the elements are right—a westering sun, glittering pond, pin on the edge, a turkey buzzard or two in majestic glide above—the founders' feel for the potential universal moment has served us well. Members and guests alike have fallen marvelously apart on the eighteenth green and shown us their naked souls.

We all agree that a glimpse of a naked soul is an essential part of what makes a club a club.

That day PJ took us further. His ball took the hump, and PJ didn't flinch ... His ball came back on line. It dropped. There was silence on the deck. PJ's putt, a brazen make-or-break attempt, made it to the hole! JR Briscoe was holding the pin. He did a little dance in celebration—barely a step and a half, then ran to the aid of our friend as he went down. GD Smart remained unaware, preoccupied with the logistics of a twelve-footer. In effect, GD missed PJ Barfard's death.

With GD Smart crouched in front of his twelve-footer, oblivious, JR Briscoe was the only one of us who realistically might have taken a detailed read of the final things in PJ's eyes. Yet the more we explore it, the more JR has become an extraneous witness to the fact of PJ's dying. Realism and death do not stay together long in the collective mind; no, there's something larger there that grows. In the face of PJ's immaculate death, JR Briscoe's observations have flown off with the birds. But JR has taken this in stride.

The putt drops, PJ smiles, head tilted slightly like an inquiring dog. A dog who sees something he thinks he likes. We have discussed this; *like a dog* is now unanimously endorsed. Then he goes down— phlump, flat on his nose. And there was this one golden bird, not a finch, that appeared and settled on the head of the pin, then flew when PJ fell.

PJ's last-ever putt was a magnificent triumph. And the man dies at the moment it drops!

JR Briscoe understands that PJ Barfard's status was suddenly relative, prime material for apotheosis, the heroic thing that lies within each member's heart. But GD Smart resented the fact we didn't wait to let him putt out and finish his round before we swarmed the eighteenth green. In submitting his official protest, GD has insinuated a sentimental and therefore false sense of respect on our part for a man who was, strictly speaking, no longer even a member at the time.

Strictly speaking, yes: memberships are automatically transferred to designated heirs at the time of death, and each member must make the necessary provisions for this eventuality.

PJ had. Phil Jr. now owns PJ's card and locker.

But sentimental? GD Smart insults. GD pays his fees—but we wonder if he's truly one of us.

PJ Barfard lay there like a god, historical, a defining moment for the clubhouse wall. We saw it clearly. And, clearly, we could not sit by and watch. We left our drinks and ran. Too late, of course; it had to be too late for it to have been so sublime. We knew this, and we ran. All the members ran to join, all hearts clamouring to be a part of it.

And we stood on the eighteenth green. And we told ourselves we loved him.

Oh, PJ! We know exactly who we are.

Distance

Hamza pushes hard against the revolving doors and is caught off guard by the cold gust of wind that greets him. It's snowing outside, but after the dry stifling warmth of the metro the snowflakes melting on his nose are more of a relief than a discomfort. Hamza hasn't been in Montreal that long. It was the beginning of fall when he arrived, just over a year ago, and he fell instantly in love with the reds, browns, and yellows of the trees. They reminded him of the colours of the desert, but it was a desert suspended over his head rather than stretching beneath his feet. "Just wait till winter," people had told him. "You're going to want to leave once it starts snowing." But winter had come and gone, and he'd found that it wasn't as bad as they'd made it out to be. Sure, the slush collecting on street corners could be annoying, and the constant gloominess made you doubt that the sun existed, but watching the snowflakes fall made up for it all. Even on the coldest and windiest of days he enjoyed walking through the park and staring straight up into falling snow.

Today, however, Hamza didn't have to walk for long. The masjid, or mosque, he was going to was just across the street from the metro. Although he'd been to this area many times before, he'd never been inside the mosque. In fact, this would be his first visit to any mosque since arriving in Montreal. "Keep good strong ties with the Muslim community when you get to Canada," his grandfather had told him just before Hamza left the Middle East. "They'll be like your family there." Hamza had dutifully promised that he would, but he had never lived up to that promise. He wasn't and had never been religious, and on the rare occasions that he did think of God it was to wonder why anyone would make a world so full of poverty, hurt, and injustice. As for the Muslim community, Hamza felt that he'd be living a lie if he approached them as a fellow Muslim while knowing full well in his heart that he didn't believe.

His visit to the mosque today was more of a chore than anything else. Two days ago, Ali, an old school friend who'd also moved to Montreal, had cornered him in the university cafeteria. "After tomorrow is the first day of Ramadan. You have to come to the masjid with me," Ali had said, leaning across the grimy table littered with empty trays and plastic coffee cups. "There'll be a meal, an iftar, so we can break our fast together, and afterwards we can pray salat al tarawih. Just like when we were kids." Hamza had been reluctant and had insisted that he didn't fast or pray anymore and that he especially didn't want to take part in the hour-long prayers offered during Ramadan. But Ali didn't know how to take "no" for an answer, and in the end, to please his friend, Hamza had agreed to go.

That was Monday, and today is Wednesday. It is past six o'clock now, and the sun set over an hour ago, so the iftar is probably already over and the prayers should be starting soon. Hamza crosses the road and heads towards the masjid, and pushing open the big glass doors he steps into a carpeted square entrance. Hanging on the wall to his right is a sign that reads *Please Remove Shoes*, and all along the walls are shoe racks spilling over with footwear of all shapes and sizes. Hamza slowly takes his boots off and, making sure that they're not dripping, puts them on the top shelf of one of the shoe racks. He then walks into the adjoining room and looks around him in surprise.

This masjid is nothing like the ones he'd known back home: big domed buildings, richly decorated and, more often than not, empty, except for the weekly Friday prayer. This is little more than a room, but it's full of men and *women* standing in circles, talking, while children run between their legs laughing and screaming at each other in Arabic, French, and English. The room itself is unfurnished except for the wall-to-wall carpeting, some folding chairs resting against the back wall, and a few old bookcases.

And there, leaning against a wall near the back of a room, sits

Ali with a big book open across his lap. He's reading intently, and he doesn't notice as Hamza approaches him. "Salam Ali, what's happening?" Hamza says when he is near enough not to have to raise his voice. Ali's head snaps up and a smile spreads across his face. "You're late asshole," he says getting up quickly and punching his friend lightly on the shoulder. "I expected you to come for the food and leave before the prayer started, and here you are doing the opposite."

Hamza opens his mouth to answer, but before he has a chance to say anything the Imam calls for the start of prayers; Hamza and Ali join the rest of the men in forming rows. The women make separate rows towards the back of the room. With a sigh, Hamza resigns himself to spending the next hour struggling to remember the words to the prayers. To his right, Ali stands with his head bowed slightly, his eyes closed, and his hands folded across his stomach. His lips are already moving rapidly as he recites the first part of the prayer.

A sudden ache grips Hamza's heart in that moment, and for a second he wishes that he knew what it is like to *know* you have a purpose. Lost in his own thoughts, he forgets about the prayer and simply goes through the motions, following the lead of the rest of the congregation.

"Al Salamu Alaikum Wa Rahmat Allah, Al Salamu Alaikum Wa Rahmat Allah."

Peace be upon you and the mercy of God, Peace be upon you and the mercy of God.

As the prayer ends, Hamza and Ali each shake hands with their neighbour, then move quickly towards the exit and grab their shoes. As they step outside, a cold gust of wind greets them and Ali pulls his coat tighter around him. "Brrr ... I hate the weather in this country," he says looking up at the sky and hurrying towards the metro. Hamza smiles and looks up into the falling snow. He strains his eyes to watch the snowflakes land on the tip of his nose and melt, then hurries after his friend.

Carrie Haber

The Unsanded Balloon

The sky was a cross between film grain and toothpaste, and it made all the cows in the landscape tingle with a quiet knowledge of what was coming.

The bluegrass stage in the main barn was enclosed by a semicircle of old-timers, bent this way, crooked that way, in suspenders, tweed, crisp jeans, and flatflower dresses.

Children tumbled, tagged, and fought in the bales by the corner. Everyone else sat, stood, danced, drank, and talked about this year's crops, and this and that. Women were lined up along the back wall, raffling off thick, dry cookies, a quilt, and at least twelve sets of somewhat inspired salt-and-pepper shakers.

Outside, Wilson was flaming up his hot-air balloon for two-ticket rides. He stood in his basket, cranked his neck, and allowed himself the superb dizziness of this position, watching the fluttering silk rise. His jeans hung loosely, as did his face, giving him the stature of an old pelican that has just swallowed too big a catch. A few children had gathered to watch, and he ignored them.

"How far can it go, mister?

"How *high* can it go?"

"Can we have a ride?"

"I was here *first*."

Wilson gazed into his inflating dome, as though helpless in prayer under a chapel fresco. The flame's roar hurt his ears, and the gas and heat and rush turned everything he saw to liquid. The ground below was sopping with soda and livestock urine. A baby goat chewed the leg of the picnic table it was tied to. It paused to watch the various creatures scramble in the nearby pen: five-dollar rabbits, an oily black sheep and her offspring, adamant ducks. A sore cow, who just lay near her latest excrement in a sullen torpor, heavily blinked and chewed on something the children had passed her.

One of Wilson's little girls sat on a bench near the barn door, her pink T-shirt proud along the collarbone with prize ribbons. She hadn't looked at any other children after winning the three-legged race and popcorn-stringing contest and avoided stares as she walked away from the dunking booth where she'd successfully sunk her brother. She was famous that day, and it burned. The other children's gazes were spiked with heat; a few of the little ones had followed her from contest to contest and stood beside her as she lined up for candy. She'd heard them whisper when she passed them. Now she sat by herself in the barn, half in broken sunlight, half in the musty shadow of the barn beams. Her legs were covered in fine blond hair, mosquito bites, and scrapes. She cupped three bunnies on her lap, deflecting their every effort to jump down with her rigid, careful palms. Through the open barn door she could see her father, a ripe strawberry bulging from his basket, and did not expect him to look back. She wanted to say, "Here I am, Daddy." Or, "Look how good I am with the rabbits." Or, "Look at this poor old cow."

Wilson felt small movements all around him. Corn popping. Fifty cents being spent on things. Cigarettes being passed around by young people in bad haircuts, shivering under three or four raindrops. The thin glimmer of pinwheels under a bright grey sky. It was all the regular patter of every year's fair. Wilson could not remember it ever being different, except last year, when they invited Carla Farnham, the country singer. Everyone had been sure to be inside the barn for her afternoon performance, including Wilson, but, when Carla came in the wrong door and pushed through the crowd with her guitar case, she turned out to be fat and ended up playing bad rock covers in a featherlight strum. Today, Wilson caught the little sounds and movements around him and collected them in that hobo's kerchief part of the brain that packs these things lightly before a voyage. He imagined himself a few other people—an Italian seafarer, for example, preparing his craft with his back to the sounds of the port, the fishermen haggling with merchants, the dockworkers talking sports. The balloon slowly filled. The children that had lined up were given rides, while Wilson watched the horizons on all sides rise and fall, rise and fall.

At the other side of the fairground, there was Burton.

Burton was the kid who threw up in the trashcan behind the hot dog booth, and everybody saw—and anybody who didn't see, heard. A few families, cluttered around the picnic tables that stuck out from under the plastic canopy, were the first to see Burton standing lonely beside the trash can, like a well-trained dog caught in too many scents and not knowing which way to go. The can came up to his shoulders, and his hair was in his eyes. There was heat coming off that boy, and, if it wasn't from crying, it was from the throbs of embarrassment that wracked his little frame. There was no running water on the grounds, and Burton felt trapped under the heavy stench of his insides, in front of the whole town. He could see his parents' barn atop a far hill, ten kilometres away. He started to run for the barn, and then, like a spooked horse, changed his mind. He turned and ran right through the crowd, between the booths and the barn, and his lungs hurt.

Past the fairground, there was nothing but the centre of town, where the park was. The park, this time of day, was full of grade eights from his class.

Wilson was on his way up, teetering with the weight of the sandbags he had not yet thrown overboard. The slow and gargantuan balloon—with its red and yellow bulges against the grey, drizzling air—was a beacon of content. It was a balloon. It was nothing to be ashamed of. It told Burton so. Burton ran for Wilson and stopped at the rope-hold.

"You're too big, kid." Wilson slumped a sandbag up onto the side of the basket and told Burton to get out of the way. Burton reached up and pulled the sandbag to the ground. Wilson heaved another.

"Watch yer fingers, kid."

"I'm thir*teen*." Burton was reasoning with his left foot, as it took hold in a divet on the basket. He was not convincing Wilson of much, who clearly did not want the company. One sandbag left. Wilson kept an eye on the frantic boy, who was hyperventilating as he tried to climb into the basket.

"You got ears or no? This is going up—move it."

Burton struggled to clamber into the basket the way a waterlogged dog struggles to climb onto a raft. He had no ears, nor eyes, nor any sense except pure, cold, wholly consuming fear. He grabbed a rope and pulled himself up onto the basket ledge.

Wilson put his hands against the boy and pushed, and Burton fell to the ground with all the ceremony of the last sandbag. Wilson thrust a long flame into the balloon and began to rise, watching the people stream towards the still boy, and did not shout back. The flame hushed out the crowd's raging. Wilson turned to face the mountains—the dark, prone chain distilled into the landscape. He became smaller and smaller as he floated over them, over cows, and over any remnant wanting. He floated, and the floating inhaled him like all the other clouds.

Wilson's little girl did not watch her father disappear any longer. She stayed inside the barn for a long time, whispering promises to the rabbits.

Maranda Moses

Ritual

Don't spill the water. Don't spill the water.

Sundays are meant for the gospel, Saturdays are meant for rituals. Every Saturday I was expected to run errands for my mother. These errands included shopping at the Atwater Market. Sometimes I was expected to purchase fruits and vegetables, chicken or blade roast (not too much fat), and some special products from the West Indian store owned by Ms. Thompson.

Don't spill the water. Don't spill the water.

"Gyal, you na bring the water yet!" my mother screamed.

The water splashed. It rushed down the side of the aluminium bucket I struggled to carry, forming a large puddle on the floor. Once I reached the kitchen my mother was in plain sight watching me sternly with her hand on her hip.

"Whey wrong wid you?" she asked angrily.

"Nothing," I replied in my usual timid tone.

As she verbally fussed that I didn't have enough strength to carry a simple tub of water, she grabbed the bucket from me, causing more spillage.

Subsequent to cleaning the puddle on the floor I was commanded to go to the market to buy several items—it was Saturday after all. Here is what the list consisted of: eggs, garlic, onions, carrots, creamed coconut, cocoa butter, camfo cake.

This list was quoted to me, not written. I was to commit all the goods on the list to memory, but I couldn't recognize the last one. I had to enquire about this item—I was certain that my mother's pronunciation of the word and the actual spelling were quite different.

"Camfo cake," my mother reiterated, pronouncing it the same way again.

It made no difference to me how she pronounced it. I was still unaware of what it was. After I had asked a third time, she rolled her eyes, sighing and swearing the way only a West Indian mother can sigh and swear.

Going to the market was a task I abhorred. I enjoyed the fresh air while walking to and fro, but going on foot under the scorching hot sun was unbearable. Feeling the wrath of a fiery orange ball in the sky was overwhelming. I was absolutely positive that I had become two shades darker within the span of ten minutes. By the time I had reached the market there were many people who had invaded the stores, which were under a series of brown roofs resembling tent-like shelters. I entered the fruits and vegetable store, whose name I could not recall even though I had been going there since I was a baby. I saw the oranges fighting for a place next to the window as people picked their fruits discriminatingly. I managed to get everything on the list except for the cocoa butter, the coconut cream, and the "camfo cake"—whatever that was. Customers leaving Ms. Thompson's store struggled as they carried their bags of groceries and tried to eat their beef-filled patties—simultaneously.

Don't forget the camfo cake. Don't forget the camfo cake.

Ms. Thompson's store was crowded on a daily basis. Customers couldn't walk anywhere without knocking over a yam or a dasheen. Behind her counter at the cash register she maintained a wall of Black cosmetic products. Products that help you achieve the American standard of beauty. On the other side of the store was a wall of towering nonperishable goods—canned ackee, beans, corn, cake mix, and cookies. Towards the back of the store was a refrigerated section. It was there I spotted the coconut cream. That left the cocoa butter and the camfo cake.

Don't forget the camfo cake. Don't forget the camfo cake.

As I made my way through the aisles I noticed a group of young suspicious-looking boys in the store who were not much older than me. I was so distracted by their obnoxious behaviour that I knocked over a potato.

Don't forget the camfo cake. Don't forget the camfo cake.

The boys had put a few small boxes of tamarind in their sinking pants pockets. Ms. Thompson, oblivious to what was going on, had been busy charging and bagging products for the customers. The boys approached the gum rack near the counter, where they huddled and took up a few gum packets. The boys saw me watching them. I looked away feeling a little abashed and walked to the counter, where I waited to pay for the items I had picked up. An old man was standing by the door waiting for his wife, who was in front of me. I recognized the woman but did not know her. She on the other hand knew and remembered who I was, despite never having actually held a conversation with me.

Don't forget the camfo cake. Don't forget the camfo cake.

It was finally my turn to pay. The lady who was in front of me had not yet left the store with her husband. I asked for "camfo cake," but of course Ms. Thompson couldn't understand what I was asking for. I repeated my request in the West Indian accent I adopted from my mother, which certainly did the trick. She finally understood and turned to the wall behind her to reach for the product.

"Okay, camphor!" she repeated, to offer some reassurance to herself.

She placed the camphor in the bag. The money that remained was more than enough to pay for it. It was at that point chaos struck— the suspicious-looking boys were on the verge of leaving the store when an anonymous voice yelled out to Ms. Thompson, "Watch, the likkle boy and them a tief!"

Whoever yelled wasn't able to finish their sentence before the boys shoved their way past the old man out Ms. Thompson's store. The middle-aged pear-shaped storeowner was yelling and swearing the way all West Indian women yell and swear, and she ran out the door after the boys. She would never be able to catch up to them.

Her age and health wouldn't permit it. Everyone in the store had raced outside to stop the young boys. Others in the market had stood still and watched nosily as the boys outran every man who chased after them.

I brought the bags home to my mother, who was in the kitchen already starting on what smelled like soup. She sifted through the bags examining everything I had bought. I felt a lump in my throat as she searched for the camfo cake. She picked up the camphor and held it in the air as if to decipher it. From the expression on her face I was positive I had done something wrong. Maybe I had picked up the wrong *type* of camphor. Maybe I was supposed to buy more than just one pack. She sifted through the bag, looking voraciously. For what, I did not know. With a look of frustration on her face she stared me in the eyes and yelled, "Gyal, where the cocoa butta?"

Barry Webster

Circles

Each Friday at Paul's we play games. Charades, slap-your-neighbour, crack-an-egg-on-your-cheek. Streetlights glow gold in the darkening outside, and, giddy from cheesies and root beer (Paul's in AA, insists "no booze"), we become gloriously stupendously magnificently ridiculous. Henrietta balances on one leg, sings "Oh Amsterdam." Sam spins, blinking, chants "I'm a lighthouse, a lighthouse." I cry out, "*The Exorcist* shall rid us of the demon of lethargy," and laughter ricochets between bare walls. We fall back, the soft sofa molding perfectly to our butts. In one corner the clock hangs, and, if we remember not to look, it soon ceases to exist.

Then, one night, a new guest. Ron.

He has no lips, mouth, or nose, only glaucous globulous eyes that attach to our every move, stick like leeches to the skin, cannot be shaken off.

Our motions decelerate. Voices fade.

In my Freshie-filled whiskey glass, I see myself whole.

Ron says, "Why do you all do this? I prefer to get to know people, have meaningful talks. For God's sakes, don't you see how foolish you all look."

A bell has sounded, and Henrietta, Sam, Paul, and I gaze into each other's eyes, as half-visible clouds of whirling dust settle quietly on furniture.

Then, deflated, huddling together for warmth, we collapse onto the couch. In a new silence we soon decide that, okay, we will do it. We will talk. Very seriously. One to another.

We begin. First Paul, Nicole, myself, Sam. We share tales of childhood trauma: Paul's godmother washed his hair daily in cherry jello; Nicole was once beaten with a stale baguette; parents constantly horked out our names like phlegm. And don't forget the horrifying present: our lovers, mouldy-breathed psychopaths who coat our genitals in Shake-and-Bake and broadcast our flaws on the subway public address system; daily our workplace offices spin like crazed merry-go-rounds as colleagues vomit down mailslots, while shrieking neighbours pound on our apartment doors, landlords enclose bomb threats with rent-increase notices, and cockroaches with tap-dance heels clatter through our dreams.

The air's heavy, and we sink to the floor to suck the dirt from carpet fronds.

Ron concludes, "...and then my mother said I looked like Godzilla's excrement."

We sigh. Is that finally everything?

I stare at the bare hanging bulb for a clue what to do next. A crack in the ceiling zigzags like a frenzied, seismic graph line.

—Then an abrupt realization paints the walls neon topaz yellow: everything in the world exhausts itself. Even tragedy can't go on forever.

The carpet changes to the speckled gold of rippling wheat, the lightbulb is a silver, spinning discoball.

Sam shouts, "Cock-a-doodle-do."

Pinball-machine lights start flashing as the couch slowly reinflates. Henrietta, then Nicole, Paul, Sam, and I rise, each standing on one leg, arms flapping.

Alice Zorn

High Noon

Leaning into the curve on his bike, Carl turned east on Laurier. A fine-boned man with straight brown hair and a serious face, he kept an eye on the traffic while he thought about work. What to put on the menu. What was in the fridge. And his latest new worry, Emma.

A month ago he'd hired a new kitchen prep. She used a knife like a pro. She kept the counters tidy. She didn't chatter; she was quiet. Compared to some of the preps he'd had in his ten years as a chef, Emma was a gift. No less.

"Mushrooms," he'd say. "Halved." They were ready.

"Lime juice, about a cup." It was done.

Both slim, they moved easily between the cast-iron hulk of the stove and the stainless-steel counters. Emma peeled and chopped and rinsed. Carl stirred as butter foamed in a pan. Meat sizzled.

Once the orders started coming in, Carl handed Emma plate after plate of meat, fish, and pasta. She added olives, a sprinkle of caraway seeds, a twig of thyme.

People wanted to be fed well, but promptly too. During the week their minds were on deals and appointments. They were always in a rush at lunchtime. Here in the kitchen, though, order reigned. Or so Carl would have it.

Then, one day last week, Emma came late. Carl had to start his own prep, parboiling and peeling tomatoes, flaking flesh off a tuna—tuna with its billion, tiny bones! It wasn't even possible to work quickly.

When Emma finally walked in, she didn't even seem aware she was late. She knotted a bibbed apron around her waist, pulled her blond hair into a ponytail, and only then looked to see what he was doing. Carl waited for her to explain. She didn't.

She was on time the next day. The day after that, too.

Then yesterday: more than half an hour late. Carl finally changed the menu because he thought he was going to have to cook alone. Forget the chicken and pesto rolls. Keep it easy. Stir-fry.

By the time Emma showed up, he might as well have been alone still. It was almost 9:00!

"We need to have a talk," he said tersely, as he reached for a knife to cube eggplant.

"About what?" She waited.

"Time in the Western world." Despite his annoyance, Carl was pleased with the line—putting her lateness within a greater context. You had to be on time for work. She should know!

Without the least sign of guilt or even wonder, Emma motioned him away and took the knife. She nodded at the counter, where the chicken breasts lay, one on top of the other. "Didn't you say yesterday you were going to do rolls?"

She finished chopping the eggplant, threw a wave of salt across it, then used one hand to toss it all up while reaching for a mallet to pound the meat.

As Carl spread pesto on the flattened breasts, rolled and tied them, she ran water in the sink to clean lettuce. She saw they were low on capers and opened a fresh jar. She lay several endives on the salad table to break apart as she needed them.

By the time J-C clipped the first order in the window, they were ready. Chicken and pesto rolls, string beans roasting under an eye-level grill, ratatouille, endive, and butter lettuce.

Chantal flung the door open to ask, "Do we really not use peanut oil? Because this man says if he gets just a drop, he'll die."

Emma said lightly, "Is that called dropping dead?"

"Very funny," said Chantal. "I have to deal with him!"

Carl said, "No, but we've got peanuts in the kitchen. I can't guarantee I'm using a knife that's never chopped a peanut, so if it's a question of life or death..."

Chantal disappeared.

Once in stride, Carl always felt a calmness settle. He could cook; he only wanted to be ready.

He slid the pan of chicken rolls over a whisper of flame. He reached for an omelette pan as Emma cracked eggs into a bowl.

Slowly the orders stopped coming in. For another day people were fed and happy. Until tomorrow when it would start all over again.

Carl had prepared a salad for the staff lunch. Emma was on her way out to join the others when she stopped. "What did you say you wanted to talk about? Time in the Western world?"

Carl frowned at the stock, which still hadn't come to a boil. He assumed she'd understood. It seemed so obvious to him.

But Emma just stood there.

"Well," he said, improvising clumsily, "clocks are all set to the same time so that people know what time it is—so they won't be late."

"You think they don't know how to tell time in the East?"

"No, I meant—"

"Because they make watches in China."

He looked at her in surprise. "Sometimes you're late," he said. "You're supposed to help, not show up when I'm practically ready to do lunch alone."

"At 8:00 in the morning?" She met his look directly. "No-one's eating lunch yet. This isn't about *time*. It's about the way you work."

Leaning with her shoulder, she pushed against the door. It swung back emptily. A low bubbling sound from the stove reminded Carl of his stock. He lowered the flame and put on the lid.

He had no idea what she meant. There was nothing wrong with the way he worked. The restaurant was doing well because of how he worked. Nobody had ever questioned him.

But nobody had ever worked with him as Emma did. Not just beside him, they worked in tandem. What did she mean, *the way he worked?* He truly had no idea.

He felt offended, but he also couldn't shake the notion that Emma understood something he didn't. Her words—the knowing expression on her face—stayed with him for the rest of the day.

Steering his bike around the smashed glass in the alley now, Carl cruised to the open backdoor of the restaurant. Loud music thrummed into the cool, morning air.

He locked his bike and took the stairs two at a time. He went directly to the dining room, behind the bar, and reached for the button on the sound system.

In the kitchen Emma stood at the counter, peeling cartoon limbs of ginger. Glancing up, she arched her eyebrows. "You don't like music?"

"You can hear it outside," he said as he walked past her to get an apron.

Emma nodded. "Right. In the alley. It'll bother the deliverymen."

He didn't answer. He was relieved she was there—on time as he'd requested.

Then he saw the great mound of parsley she'd chopped and left on a board. By noon, it would be limp and useless. It was too early to chop parsley...

He turned and looked at Emma. All innocence, her head was bent over the ginger she was peeling.

Dawn Kackley

Alpha: Revelation

November 20

I have been waiting for a sign but realize now that it has been here, living and breathing beside me, for almost two months. I know God has not forsaken me, because He has sent me Boris.

Aside from the existence of the animal, a wonderful beast who forgives me every day, I stop and think: it would be wrong to buy cat food, to feed a dumb animal when people are without sustenance. So I eat less and feed Boris from my regular portions. If there were no God, I might have found a dog at my door. I believe things are changing.

Today I dressed up and tried out to be Santa Claus. They did not seem to see the mark upon my forehead, I am quiet and well brought up, perhaps these things will make a difference and I will get the job.

Yet I am afraid of this. I need the work, but I am afraid to look at all of those young faces, expecting something from me, all of those young faces that I cannot help. I am Santa Claus! Tonight I pick up the suit, and next Saturday I go to Fairview Shopping Centre. Ho ho ho!

A hollow laugh, perhaps, because I cannot help but feel this is a double test. How much can I bear so that I may gain redemption? I will be surrounded by children, each one alive, surely a tremendous torture. And then, too, to be Santa Claus: this secular icon can only represent our greed. Perhaps I am meant to open people's eyes to this evil. Yes, yes, this must be my chance for forgiveness!

December 2

Child child child child child becomes children children children

children CHILDREN. Sounds like brother and brethren, a very old plural form, but these are from a new millennium. What hope is there for them? Yet, as long as they live, there must be hope.

I keep seeing the dead one but try to do as I must.

Little boy sits on my knee. I smile at him like any cherry-nosed old Santa, growing wrinkles as I look into his hopeful greedy eyes. "Santa," he says. Not more than five years old. "I want a Pokemon V-Trainer for Christmas." I look at Mom and Dad smiling proudly, maybe a tear in the eye of Mom standing just a step or two back from the boy. I smile, too, and talk over the child's head to Mom and Dad. "Of course, son!" I say, loud enough for the beaming parents to hear. "I'll bring you all of the Pokemon toys! Every single one! And all of their accessories!" (I would name all of the accessories, but I don't know what they are.) The little boy gives me a huge grin and hops off my lap. His parents stare at me, puzzled, then angry.

This, I believe, will make them reflect. Why do they bring him here if this isn't what they want? I am merely trying to earn my forgiveness, to open the eyes of the parents and to save this new generation.

Tuna again tonight, since it's one of Boris's favourites. I would have named him Morris, after the cat in the old commercial, but he had a cold when I found him. That was my own little joke.

December 4
I've taken to reading the circulars in the newspaper to bone up on the new toys, and now I promise every boy over seven a Nintendo. The children's delight plucks at the thin fabric of my soul. "Nintendo! Super Smash Brothers!" The storeowners should be happy, too. Why else do they want me there?

December 6
Woke up this morning in a sweat sticky as blood. The dreams are back, that young face, me with nothing to give. Still I must go back

to being Santa Claus for the families, I must try to teach them, as I have been shown.

December 8

Mall Manager came over to stick a hot sting in Santa's ear today. Parents complaining. "Shape up or ship out!" Ho ho ho. They don't want what I'm trying to give them, but after the dream I am even more intent on redeeming myself. I spread the word about Nintendo, Hogwarts Castle, Babblin' Boo.

The pain is mine. They must see.

December 9

Even Alpha and Omega were silent babies until they grew up into uttered sentences, and then they became All! I have been forgiven, I have rejoined humanity.

Santa Claus was defrocked today. Mall Manager came to me at break and said, *Remove your uniform immediately. Go to the mall washroom. Undress and turn in your uniform now!*

I got the key and walked down that dark hallway that leads to the washroom, feeling suddenly weighted by the false pregnancy of my belly-pillow. Had I ruined it? Had I failed, aborted my only chance at forgiveness? Surely, I hadn't yet received a sign that I had been welcomed back.

I turned the corner to the men's room and found the edge of my world peeled away to reveal something from one of my dreams. There, sitting on the cold, hard cement floor, was a mother nursing her baby. Her breast was bare but gently covered by a tiny mouth and groping hands, curtained by long, thin hair hanging down across her face and shirt front.

How did she get in here? She looks up at me with those same empty eyes, and in a flash she is the girl's mother; I can see the metal skin of my car smacking the thin, mortal skin of the child, and I see the mother cradling that child, looking up at me with those eyes, empty eyes. I have nothing to give her. I look again at the mother and baby, and I know I am looking at one of my own.

The caged light above her sheds the dim light of a star. I am elated but frightened, for I must ease her suffering.

I stand there alone with the mother and child. What have I to give? Very slowly, I undo my Santa Claus belt and let it drop to the floor. She is watching me carefully, and for a minute she looks afraid. I smile at her and reach up under my shirt to pull at my soft Santa belly, tugging the pillow free. I touch her shoulder gently, and she obliges me by leaning away from the wall. I slide the cushion down behind her, and as she leans back it billows softly around her neck.

The mother looks up at me, and in an instant as quick as death she redeems me with a pure, radiant smile. "Santa Claus," she says. "Merry Christmas."

I am looking at every Madonna and Child.

Brett Schaenfield

Fetishize

Frith Street was always crowded with runoff from Old Compton. Theatregoers, tourists, police looking hopelessly awkward, asses in leather, bikers in tow. Much of this spectacle could be observed from the small sidewalk terrace at Bar Italia.

Vincent squinted; flecks of sunlight reflected off the checkered sliver table. The waitress smiled at him.

"Italiano, si?" She asked.

"No," he said curtly. "Americano."

He rifled through his bag to find a notebook. A hand slapped his shoulder.

"Darling!"

"Christ, Jonas!"

"Sorry, sorry, sorry."

He signaled the waitress and sat down.

"Look at her," he said with effeminate indignity, motioning subtly towards a lean, thirtyish man sitting at the café across the street. "Met her last Tuesday at the V&A. Now she doesn't know me. Sculptor, happily married. Twins no less. Takes it up the shitters like everyone else."

Jonas smiled and waved blithely. The man grinned nervously, stood up, and went inside.

"Don't start, Jonas."

Jonas raised his voice slightly. "Hairy little biscuits! Honestly..."

"Not everyone wears their dick on their sleeve."

Jonas sighed, clasped his hands, and smiled. "So, how are we?"

"Deadlines. I really have to start that fetishism piece. Nicola wants it by Friday."

"Darling, have you ever heard of B.U.L.K.? It's quite the scene."

"Yeah, Bull took me a couple of weekends ago. I kept getting cruised by these enormous feedbags who looked like they'd just as soon chew me up as fuck me."

Vincent looked up at the sun. The waitress came to take Jonas's order.

"Speaking of which, how are things *down there*?" asked Jonas.

"This piece has been on my mind a lot. I haven't really been thinking about it."

"You're a lousy liar, darling. Everyone thinks about it. When was the last time you had a good fuck?"

"Not counting income tax?"

The waitress arrived with the coffee. She and Jonas exchanged greetings.

"I'm not looking anymore," said Vincent absently. "I've been thinking about getting a dog."

"Heavy petting is hardly a substitute. Vince. What you *need*," said Jonas, turning his attention towards a muscular bike courier who had just sat down next to them, "is to rid yourself of all those dreadful spermatozoa."

The courier smiled and nodded hello to Jonas, whose eyes, fixed squarely on his Lycra shorts, quickly darted upwards. He turned back to face Vincent and lowered his voice. "Ach, those loins. God, I love couriers."

"What, no package jokes?"

"Let's hope not, for my sake."

Jonas picked up his cup, kissed Vincent on both cheeks, and turned to face the courier.

Vincent looked around. Across the street, an obese man was wiping his lips as his partner slumped back in his chair contentedly.

Jonas was busy arranging a convenient time to meet the courier for dinner. The man stood up, handed Jonas a piece of paper, and left to unchain his bicycle. Jonas spun around to resume his conversation. "Where were we?"

"You whore."

"Were we looking at the *same* courier? Jesus..."

"I'm straight, Jonas, remember?"

"You're a hetero queer, darling. World of difference. Besides, what if it had been a woman? What would *you* have done?"

"Things don't work the same way in the straight world."

"Of course they do. You just need to be more assertive." He waved the piece of paper proudly and pulled out a pair of sunglasses. The two sat silently together watching the sidewalk.

"You should meet my friend Mia," said Jonas.

"Why?"

"You'd love her. She's a curator. Really interesting girl. Went to Oxford. Massive tits."

"Really. How massive?"

"You can barely see her face."

"Sounds a bit cerebral."

Jonas smiled and finished his coffee.

Vincent packed his things and stood up. He pulled out a crumpled five-pound note from a side pocket. "There's a film I want to see at the Curzon." He paused and looked back across the street. The two large men noticed him staring and smiled slyly. "*À bout de souffle,*" he said absently, slowly turning back to Jonas. "*Breathless...*"

He threw his bag over his shoulder and handed Jonas the money. "I'll shout for coffee today."

"That's very big of you."

"Not at all," said Vincent. "It's my pleasure."

Carolena Gordon

Shoe Salesman

I am a shoe salesman. People think that this is not glamorous work, but it is.

I work at Berlini Shoes. We sell only fine-quality Italian shoes and, of course, matching handbags, evening bags, and assorted leather goods. Only the best, and to a good clientele. I open the store every day at 9:30 a.m. That sounds early, but I use the time between 9:30 and 11:00, while both my boss Domenic and the first clients of the day trickle in, to note the most recent trends in shoe fashion and style. Berlini's has a great Gaggino espresso machine, and I make myself a double every morning before I slide into a low leather chair to take in the morning fashion show. The café across the mall corridor is the only one open for lattés and croissants before lunch, and it is filled with the very latest in foot fashion and accessories.

My name is Marcus Mitchell Robson, but here at Berlini's I am just "Marco." Domenic is actually Donald, but when he took over Berlini's from its previous owner, Enzo Fierimonte, six years ago he decided that all the salesmen would be Italian because everybody loves to hear an Italian accent when they are paying $300 for a genuine imported Italian shoe. Enzo was the last real Italian to ever work at Berlini's. Ever since Domenic has hired guys like me and told us to fake the accent and stuff a sock down our pants if we have to, just so long as we make like we're Italian for the clients.

Domenic hired me four years ago after a two-minute interview. He asked me precisely three questions in his ridiculous Italian accent, which fooled me completely: "Are you what they call a morning person?"; "Do you know that women's shoes come in different widths?"; "Have you ever been arrested for stealing?"

Once I had answered yes to the first two questions and no to the third, "Marco" was born. After parading me around the store to perfect my macho swagger and discreetly determining that I would not need the sock, Domenic decided that I was ready for retail. Within a week I was opening the store, wiping down the shelves, and arranging the window displays to highlight the new merchandise and feature it in the appropriate seasonal themes. The latter talent was a gift for Domenic as he usually paid a design student $100 to do the displays once a month. When I started rearranging the shoes and handbags in the store during the after lunch slow period in my first week Domenic said: "Hey Marco, what are ya? Gay or what?"

He hiked up his pants and adjusted himself while he said this, and his chin shot out daring me to answer. Gino (a.k.a. Grant), one of the other salesmen, sipped his espresso and smiled politely at Domenic's joke. No-one thinks Domenic is funny, and everyone thinks he takes the Italian thing a little too far, but he pays us okay and frankly he is just weird enough to make you not want to piss him off. I smiled at Domenic, mimicked his adjustment gesture, and said in my newly minted accent: "You wish, Dom. You wish."

There was dead silence for a split second, during which I saw Gino freeze. Domenic waited a moment, laughed out loud, and then looked at me with the eyes of a seasoned killer and answered: "You are one fuckin' asshole Marco. Go crazy!"

And, with that, I became Berlini's display man.

Once I became a shoe salesman, beautiful and wealthy women and very successful men suddenly depended upon my expertise as the Mediterranean marvel in fashion and design. I slipped sleek shoes on their feet and buffed the leather to a fine glow, selling pair after pair. With authority I had them march around the store the way that Domenic had marched me around that first day. I imparted the wisdom of purchasing expensive well-made shoes from my homeland in a careful and flawless Italian accent. I whispered upcoming sales into their willing ears and whisked expensive shoes onto their willing feet while Domenic suggested accessories. We were the dynamic duo of shoes and leather accessories.

In the past four years my expertise has grown and Domenic's wallet has, too. A slew of young "Italians" with exotic names like "Vito" and "Francesco" have joined us and left us while Domenic has become more eccentric. Two years ago he began to insist that we always speak to each other in our adopted accents, and he has recently taken to cursing in Sicilian, although it is clear that he has no clue what he is saying. A while ago I heard him call Pietro (a.k.a. Peter) a big bowl of unholy clams in a cream sauce while he lectured him on how to sell accessories. I suppressed a laugh as Domenic stomped into the back room. I heard a loud bang, which later turned out to be the sound of Domenic throwing a $500 men's loafer at the back door, leaving a menacing black mark on the door as a reminder of his unpredictability.

Berlini's is well situated on the ground floor of a mall that joins four office towers housing the city's investment bankers, lawyers, and other miscellaneous professionals. They have everything Berlini's needs: money, the absence of time in which it can be spent, an awareness of what is in fashion, and a remarkable sense of entitlement to smart leather goods.

I first saw her on a cold October morning while I sipped my espresso and eyed the passing footwear. The front of Berlini's allows for a view of the café and down the hall in two separate directions. All of which provide me with a great deal of footwear to consider. I had just sized up a smart pair of emerald green loafers on an 8B with foot fat that was unfortunately quite aesthetically displeasing to the trained eye. I may not have been in this business for long, but I do know that a good shoe cannot fix a bad foot.

I heard her before I saw her. The muted sound of her leather heels on the slate tile sounded like the click of a slow clock; it was that regular. She was a beautiful and perfect 7AA with sculpted ankles and an impeccable arch. I could tell this immediately from the steel-blue sling backs that she was wearing. They were a fine-quality Italian leather, but a style I had never seen at Berlini's. Her purse was a perfect matching blue clutch with a silver clasp. Feminine, yet professional—and that is a tough standard to meet. She stopped to order her coffee at the café. While she waited, her right shoe wrapped itself around her left ankle and rubbed the side of her ankle gently, rhythmically until her coffee was finally delivered to her. She slipped her clutch purse under her left arm and gracefully turned and glided down the hall to the bank of elevators that lifted her towards a world unknown to me.

First Light

The old porch quilt held Iris together, and Iris held the container of coffee close to her chest. Just a touch of brandy, she reasoned. Stan won't taste it.

She set out towards the south field, back where the kids' swing used to be. It seemed as if just a month ago this land was swaying like so many golden feathers. But the hay was cut, and winter came. The stars were starting to dim now, and sunshine that was falling on the Great Lakes (still so very far away) was giving the snow on their land a blue hue. Iris approached the pulsing embers of a coal fire burning on a patch of exposed hard grey soil. For two nights her boys fed that fire under a moonless sky, occasionally checking their father's wooden face for direction.

When Iris reached her husband's side, he glanced eastward and spoke. "First light. Pastor's wife should be up."

Daniel shook off his sooty gloves and whispered, "I'll take you, Ma." As he walked past, the boy laid the pick axe at his father's feet.

Stan took the coffee from Iris and held her with his eyes for a moment. She looked over at the barn and walked steadily towards the truck. Too long to wait to commit a child to the ground, she thought. Much too long. But land allows for only persistent men— God must have made it so to keep us as far from Hell as possible.

Stan crouched to the ground and dragged the axe over the soil causing the black ash to fall from the embers and freckle the air with sparks. He pulled up an old, brown corn shoot near his boot, broke off the end, and stuck it in his mouth.

"You boys go on and get the shovels, now. Ground's starting to yield."

"Yes sir," they answered. Jim, now the oldest, stayed behind, not able to follow and not yet ready to lead. Since Buddy was gone, Jim couldn't find his place.

Stan straightened up and said, "You're going to have to help me fetch Buddy from the barn after we get this hole done. Can you do that, son?"

Sobered by the softness in his father's voice, Jim looked over at the barn, dark against the navy sky. When they were little, Buddy had told him that, from their bedroom window, the barn looked like a ghostly head. The two loft windows and the crooked, creaking door made a sinister face. Jim said he was cracked and wouldn't look at it, but really he didn't like it when Buddy tried to scare him. Since then, Jim would only go into the barn at night with the dog. These last few days Pepper stayed in the barn, watching over Buddy's body.

The boy tensed his lip to keep it steady. "Yes, sir. I can do it."

Stan looked at Jim's boots. "Good, son. Now get after Little Pete and help with the shovels."

"Yes, sir."

It wasn't seeing Buddy's boots that got to Stan—Jim had been wearing them since he started back at school in the fall. It was the mark they left in the snow as Jim lumbered off to the shed. It had been Buddy's job to check the fields before coming in at night. Sometimes a young cow would get forgotten down by the slough, so he would take Pepper out and walk up to the ridge for a look around. Stan called it "taking in the land" and enjoyed the thought of his son's growing pride. He would check for Buddy's fresh footprints leading up to the house before settling into bed.

Those footprints, thought Stan. My son's.

Jim stumbled and fell rounding the house on his way to the shed and stopped to cinch his boots up tighter. Inside the long, musty shed, Little Pete stirred up the cold dust that had settled on Iris's garden tools.

"We better bring something for them coals," said Jim. Little Pete emptied the wheelbarrow in silence, acting like he was in trouble.

Jim took the spades from the ground and placed them in the wheelbarrow, and the two boys walked back to their father, heads down, watching their boot laces jump from side to side.

Pepper's head lifted suddenly from the hay pile and looked outside. He whined at Buddy's coffin and, getting no response, circled the box twice before appearing at the barn door. Surrounded by glowing snow and expiring clouds of breath like far off steam engines, Stan and the boys started to dig the hole. Pepper cocked his head and sat watching them, occasionally returning to circle the coffin.

Snow squeaked under the truck as Iris and Daniel pulled up beside the house. Pepper backed up into the shadow just inside the barn.

"That silly beast hasn't eaten a thing in days. Go fetch a pat of suet from the cellar for him, would you, son?"

"Yes, Ma."

"Then you're all to come inside—I'm fixing some bread and eggs. Tell your father the hole can wait. Pastor Willis won't be here until noon."

"I will." Daniel took the matches and the lamp from the shelf in the porch and stomped down the stairs, scattering the few pests that had crept indoors. He kept the lamp with him to go out to the barn so that Pepper wouldn't growl at him. That dog has lost his tame, thought Daniel. But, as he approached the doors, the boy's nerve gave up and he threw the suet into the dark.

Stan heard Pepper's deep barking and looked towards the barn. He saw a boy running, and for a moment his heart went as still as a woodpile.

"Ma says to leave the digging and come inside. The pastor," Daniel gasped, "he's not coming till noon, Ma says."

"Noon." Stan took a bit to catch up to what he heard, then dumped the coals back into the hole. "Alright, then. Noon." He looked up at the paling sky. Some of the brightest stars were flickering with their last bit of light. "Morning's coming fast now, eh, Bud?"

The boys shot glances at one another.

"Yes, sir," they offered slowly as their father led them back to the house. Lagging behind, Little Pete heard Pepper whimpering from inside the barn. He knew his brother's body was in there, but he didn't know enough to be scared. There were many times a hay pile proved to be the safest place to hide from older brothers.

"Pepper Girl. Hey, Pepper Girl!" The dog licked the boy's face. Little Pete made himself a pile and curled up. "Good night, Buddy." Pepper sniffed at his shoes and settled in beside Pete.

"Jim, where's your brother at?"

"He's in the barn, Pa."

"Petie's got no good sense," Daniel said to his mother as she pulled his wool pants off. "That dog's gone mad, that's what I say."

"Stan. Stan, did you hear that? Go get that boy out of the barn."

He stood in the porch, looking out the window. What are they on about? The hole's not dug.

Loss/Survival

The torment always began in the same way. Treading water. Hands held behind his back by slimy entanglements of seaweed that had sprung from nowhere and caught at his wrists. The slithering, snaking coils then in large circling movements lashed themselves around his ribs, tight, tighter, forcibly expelling his breath from him, choking him, wooing him to join them in the nether reaches of their existence. Furiously he would retaliate to their languorous embraces, his legs kicking out to shake off the seaweed, to keep his head above the bone-numbing water. He knew the sweat flowed freely—chilling sweat, the sweat of fear. Then, suddenly, a burst of flame illuminated the sky, followed by a reverberating roar of sound. Next he felt rather than saw a creeping heavy darkness, spreading above and out over the vast expanse of water where he struggled alone. And then the rain began, a slow drizzle of objects, somersaulting in slow motion before plunking and plopping into the water around him. He did not understand why he was there, witnessing this strange deluge. But the unknown was imbued with fear, and he felt that he was witnessing something dreadful.

He looked up, legs moving constantly, and recognized a teddy bear, falling directly from above him. It was Kala's, named Teddy Sinha, always in her embrace, even as she said a tearful goodbye to him at the airport. Seeing Teddy, he remembered how Kala had generously offered her companion to him; she had understood that Pramod would be very lonely without her, but he had convinced her that Teddy would feel very sad if she left him behind, whereas he, her father, could be brave for the two weeks that they would be apart. He could not understand what Teddy was doing up above him. Perhaps Kala had changed her mind after all! Once again he tried to unravel his hands, to catch Teddy, to save him from the swirling mess. As he wrestled the seaweed, something drifted towards him, bright yellow bobbing cheerfully in the blackness of the water, a forlorn lifejacket, and with it, suddenly, the situation became clear.

"Daddy," he heard a call. Terror took his breath. "Daddy, look, look up at me." It was Kala, floating slowly, down towards him. "Daddy, Daddy, I'm flying, I'm Wendy, look, I'm Wendy." Her chubby arms were stretched out and moving, slowly, contrasting with the swift hammering of his heart, up and down, up and down, each movement bringing her closer to him, but she did not seem to notice this. "I'm flying off to Never-Never-Land. Bye-bye, Daddy." She waved to him.

"Kala, not now baby, not ... now!' Pramod he screamed with all his being. "Oh God," he beseeched. The lifejacket mocked him! "Come to Daddy, look at Daddy," he called. Desperately he tried to move, so that he would be under her. Break her fall. She paid no attention to him, moving her arms up and down, flying her deadly flight. He was losing the tug-of-war with the seaweed and was once again being pulled under. He did not give up. He continued to struggle, to get under her, but he only managed a strangled groan. "Kala," was all that came out before his head went under. When he surfaced Kala was nowhere in sight.

Before he could dive under in search of Kala, something splashing down in the water distracted him temporarily. A book. He glimpsed the name of its author—Kafka—as it bobbed among the other objects and then drifted out of reach. He could hardly breathe, dread filling him as he forced himself to look up. His stomach was in knots, for there was Alpana, his eldest daughter, arms outstretched in front of her, as if in a graceful dive, heading like a missile for the water. Barely a second before she reached it, she turned towards him and whispered, "Daddy," and then she, too, was lost to the depths with him a helpless spectator. His legs no longer threshed the water. They were too tired, frozen, heavy. He gave in to the pull that was taking him below. The water was now up in his ears, covering his eyes. He closed them for a split second before looking up one last time. He had no will to resist now that his daughters were in the deep. Against the deepening blackness there was a flash of gold. Oh no! He recognized Charu's beautiful wedding sari, its bright, glorious red background, scarcely visible because of the gold embroidery that wove through it. No, no, not Charu also. Sobs wracked his body.

This time it was he who called out, his voice hoarse with hysteria: "Charu, Charu." As always, the sari billowed in the wind and the anchal swathed the head and hid the face. But he knew for certain that it was Charu, because of the sari. "Charu, look at me, please, turn your head, I beg you, oh Charu," he sobbed again, putting all the force and strength he had left into his voice, fighting the water, fighting the ropes of seaweed that still held his limbs prisoner. And this time, for the first time, she turned and looked at him and smiled, illuminating her face. Miraculously, his arms came free, his legs steered like the tail of a fish, and he moved towards her, crashing, bounding desperately through the water, all the while looking up to keep her in sight. As she floated closer, she continued smiling, never uttering a word. Then he offered her his arms, and she floated into them.

"Pramod," she said in a whisper as she settled into his proffered embrace. He did not tell her about the girls, and he hoped she would not ask for them. He wanted this moment, to hold her with a fierce grip, willing himself bound to her, forever, before he went down for his daughters.

In his sleep, Pramod stretched his arm and brushed the spot that Charu filled, but he was met instead by the cool emptiness of the bedsheet. His eyes flitted open, not believing his fingers. He wondered where Charu was. Then his cheek rubbed against the familiar cold wetness of his pillow. And suddenly he was wide awake to the nightmare that he had relived once again. Except that this time he had not jumped out of bed at the end of the torment, screaming the names of his wife and children—yet masochistically grateful for the opportunity to see his children in movement. Neither did he run down for the bottle and with it wander into Alpana and Kala's rooms looking at the mementos that only served to emphasize their absence, to pour over the albums of his life, until the first light broke through night's cover and rescued him for the mechanics of living in the barren day that stretched ahead.

This time he lay still and closed his eyes, treasuring Charu's smile as she had whispered his name, for this time he had seen her face, one more time, and with the memory he let sleep overtake him.

F. Colin Browne

An Entire Family of Crickets Were Spending the Summer in a Nest Made of Twigs and Leaves and Wire

An entire family of crickets were spending the summer in a nest made of twigs and leaves and wire. The nest had been manufactured by a young boy of about thirteen. His sweatpants were torn. In school, he had learned about nests and the proper way to build them, but he would tend to go against this grain in his construction. The nest which housed the crickets was triangular in shape and the boy had taken the liberty of dying all the twigs purple and the leaves gold. He also decided to include a retractable roof made of plexiglass. Do not ask him where he managed to obtain the plexiglass, but, if you did, he would probably tell you that it was a gift, or that he had stolen it from his friend's dad.

One afternoon, the boy was playing softball with his parents. His mom was pitching. He was playing centrefield. The boy had begun to daydream. Right about now, he was mulling over the irony in the word *softball*. The ball was very hard, and *soft*, he had learned, was the opposite of *hard* (*opposite* of course, meaning something which holds properties in stark contrast to another in a similar field— *up* is the opposite of *down*, and so on). He had just begun thinking about his friend Arthur's brother when this so-called *soft*ball came zipping straight towards him, compliments of a healthy swing from his father, who held the bat, who stood at the plate, which was actually a rock. The ball hit the boy in the nose, and he fell to the ground. His mother rushed to his side and stood over him. She did not want to move him because she had seen on the TV that it was risky to move an injured person for fear of worsening the affliction. Though he was bleeding. The boy got up before his mother could touch him, and she was relieved. She was proud of herself for not attempting to sit him up or turn him over, especially given her condition.

The boy had removed his shirt and pressed it against his face to help stop the bleeding. His shirt had been a gift from his friend Arthur's brother. Arthur's brother was seventeen years old and played the trombone. Once, about a year ago, Arthur's brother was out of town. The boy, who at the time had only just turned twelve, was visiting Arthur at his parent's cottage. The two friends were playing word games until they started trying on Arthur's brother's old clothes.

Arthur's brother's old clothes all had interesting designs on them and were, more often than not, ripped or frayed.

The shirt that most intrigued our boy of twelve was a bulky, green, long-sleeved crew-neck make which had seen better days— *better* if you consider its current condition as *worse*. The boy tried on the shirt. Arthur yelled at him to take it off, but he would not. Arthur yelled at him some more. The boy spat at Arthur and then buried his toys in the mud after Arthur had run crying like a boy to his parents, who were visiting another family in another cottage. The boy stood alone amidst a large pile of Arthur's brother's clothes with no Arthur, no Arthur's brother, and no Arthur's brother's parents in sight. The shirt had a picture of a window with a dark-haired girl looking through it. She looked very sad, and her eyes did nothing to conceal it. Not that they should. Eyes are certainly not closed doors after all.

The boy cooked up some eggs, which he left on the table for when Arthur returned.

He ran home with the shirt, the very shirt that right about now was spinning with vigour inside a washing machine, a washing machine that was doing its best to cleanse the shirt of its blood-soakededness.

Arthur had decided never to speak to the boy again. He had been wholly disturbed by the plate of eggs the boy had left for him and told all his schoolmates about it. Some of them beat the boy up and ripped the pages from his textbooks and tore the straps from his bookbag. He was lucky they didn't shave his head again.

As he stared at the washing machine, our boy thought of a few things. He thought about what it must look like inside the washing machine right now. He wondered where the blood would go. He listened to the hum of the machine and to the rain against the window. His parents were listening to music in the room above him and did what he assumed was dance around the room, on the floor which creaked. He didn't wonder what it must look like inside the room, though. He knew he could find out by opening the door. He could never see inside an active washing machine, at least, not exactly.

He wasn't panicking, but his heart was beating faster; he felt removed. His body, with all its insides spinning around and over each other, began to *feel* like a washing machine, but still he couldn't see inside.

When he came to, he was bleeding. His mother was standing over him. His father stood in the distance. The boy had fallen face first onto the floor and had reinjured his nose. The floor was a concrete, basement make. His parents were smart not to move him, or so they thought. The boy had lost an awful lot of blood from his nose and really should have been taken to the hospital. One of his teeth had cracked, leaving sharp edges.

Slowly, the boy began to stand himself up using the washing machine as a crutch and, staggering just a little, fell to one knee. As he fell, he crushed his triangular nest and killed most of the crickets, the majority of which would have been spared had he not forgotten to put the retractable roof back on. but it didn't matter anyway because the crickets were made of pretzels!

As the spinnings of the washing machine came to a rest, the boy reached in and removed his shirt. Arthur's bother's shirt. He pressed it against his face to stop the bleeding as his father picked up an old broken record player, asking the boy if he would like to put the record player in the washing machine and see what might happen. The boy grabbed the record player and threw it in his mother's direction. There was a crash as it struck an old bookcase, upon which a photograph of Arthur at his kindergarten graduation had been enhanced to a disproportionately large size and framed. The boy would tell you that he had stolen this picture from Arthur's living room and had taken it to a copy centre to make alterations.

At the very second the record player crashed into the wall, Arthur was hit in the face with a softball and his mother gave birth. His father broke a wine glass. The young boy embraced his parents, and they assured him everything would be okay and that he had been born. He loved his parents very much and felt terrible for subjecting them to all that bleeding.

Rachel Mishari

Al

The ad in *The Gazette* had read simply: *Estate Sale. 1000s of Books. Absolutely No Early Birds.* Nevertheless, there they were at the door an hour early, as she knew they would be; but much quieter— remarkably much quieter than usual. None of the horsing around, none of the irrepressible bonhommie which often enough resulted in neighbouring tenants opening their doors and telling them to shut the fuck up or they'd call the police and shut the sale down. But soon the foot-shuffling, awkward last moments of jockeying for position as the earliest arrivals asserted their right to first entry, taking off their coats and putting on their glasses, readying their canvas shopping bags and backpacks as the door swung finally open and the piles of books came into sight. *Badinage*—that was Al's word for it, wasn't it?—the rising, chuckle-filled murmuring of the dealers who were about to get something for nothing; the contained excitement of the grave-robber, the ambulance-chaser. A *clutch* of book-pickers. *A murder of crows.*

More than anything, he would have loved to have been the first in line. Who other than he would have known where the real treasures lay—the true firsts with their jackets intact; complete sets with bindings firm, not a hinge loose, the whole offering clean and tight and uninscribed. All the printing numbers ranged neatly in their line like good little soldiers. The price unclipped on the flyleaf. Ideally, Mint. Preferably unread.

No, no—he'd be horrified, devastated. Ten years of picking, and his whole collection gone in ten minutes for a buck a book. And to the likes of those dealers about to shoulder their way into his house and suck up his stock as if it meant nothing but *a good find* or something they could *use at the shop.* What was it about his absence that so clarified memory: how many *good finds* was she sitting on top of? How many *good days* and *not-so-good days* were about to find their way into the various shops, marked up tenfold and wrapped in Mylar, or consigned to the fifty-cent bins or just left splayed in piles in the dust on the floor, spines broken, pages unglued, dead?

Not that there was much floor. Elsa sat cross-legged in the middle of the room on a pile of books a dozen layers deep. The police had found Al's body in the one area of the apartment he had left for himself, lying fully dressed with a package of cigarettes in one hand, the cat curled into the space between his other arm and his body. Had he lit that cigarette—the police pathologist had said this casually, dropping his own smoke into the dregs of a takeout coffee—the whole building would've gone up.

Both of the dead lay where they'd fallen asleep: *unmarked,* Elsa thought, correcting the assessment as the image of Al's face under the muted lights in the viewing room at the morgue came to her— *slightly sunned, but otherwise fine.* She hadn't seen him in, what, well over a year: not since the girls had stopped their monthly visits claiming that there was never any food at the apartment, no place to sit once they were there, and nothing to do with him anyway because he preferred not to go outside except to the sales.

It was strange to look upon a face at once so familiar and so foreign: the marriage had gone so well for the first years. She'd kept on at the library while he worked at getting his degrees and cared for the girls. And hadn't it been she who first suggested he buy one of the duplicates offered for sale by the library? What he'd wanted had been out on a two-week loan, and they'd been chatting at the counter—flirting, really—and he'd gone over to the trolley and taken a marked-up copy of one of the Greek Classics and told her that his name was Alcibiades and that he had not told anybody his real name since first grade, when his teacher tripped up on at least half of the syllables and the whole class burst out laughing. But Elsa had liked his name, and Elsa and Alcibiades fell in love and moved in together and had two children.

And Elsa, on her own side of the counter, Dewey-decimalled her pristine volumes, applied barcodes and magnetic strips, glued in the borrower pockets, purple-stamped the library logo on every available surface, then organized her universe of books alphabetically by Author and Subject and handed them out to anybody who asked— all the while teaching Alcibiades how to remove cellotape residue with lighter fluid, pencil markings with artgum, and ink with bleach. She showed him how to read the copyright page and the colophon page; she alerted him to the remainder sales and the author signings; she kept him up to date on the prizes and awards and let him know whose books were always called for and whose were culled. In short, and quite unwittingly, out of love she created a monster, deprived her children of a father, and lost forever, like a misshelved magazine, her husband of ten years.

For his part, Al left the university and turned his love of Literature and the Classics into plastic shopping bags full of buck-a-book books, which he took up to the local bookshops to trade for the money he needed to pay his rent and buy his food. But as he got better at collecting, as he rode his bicycle with bigger saddlebags, as he got to the yard sales and garage sales, the library sales and estate sales, as he began to phone the folks who advertised in *The Gazette* that they were leaving the country and had a variety of household goods for sale, Al began to build more shelves and fill them, double-row the shelves, pile the books on the floor, in the bathroom, in the kitchen, in the spaces meant for windows, beds, cold food, and hot suppers until every wall and window and floor surface was sandbagged a dozen books deep. A bunker of books. A wall-womb of books. The book-pickers' motherlode.

He no longer washed. For all other ablutions he went to the local restaurants. The books he had consigned to the freezer to rid them of mildew and mould had frozen into place. The books meant to dry their damp out in the oven remained there underneath the stacks on top of the stove itself, the water heater, and what was once used as a garbage can. He slept, as Elsa found out when she understood that the devolvement of Al's estate had fallen, by default, to her, in the middle of the middle of the room, geographically speaking, in a declivity reached by a series of meandering steps, made entirely of books.

She felt particularly sad about the cat—not so much that it had died, but that, when she had given it to Al after their breakup, she had meant it as a kind of sop for the emotional void surely he would have suffered in her absence and in the absence of the girls. When the police opined that perhaps the cat had somehow depressed the lever on the stove that released the lethal gas, or perhaps had caused to fall one of the books on top of the stove, Elsa agreed it was all possible, very possible, for the obvious assessment would have been in the realm of suicide, and how could a mother of two little girls tell her children that their father had taken his own life? She couldn't. She wouldn't. So, therefore, he hadn't.

And what better revenge—the idea had formed surprisingly quickly over the course of the days from the discovery of the body to its cremation and encasement in a little black plastic box—than to recruit a small legion of library workers to catalogue and properly evaluate, to price and restack all of the thousands of books that had become, de facto, her rightful inheritance and the shining future of her girls.

So she sat where she sat and listened to the badinage, reverential though it was, until the very second the little hand got to where it was supposed to get. Then she opened the door.

2003-2004

Kick

I was seven years old when I suddenly realized that very young babies were being flung into the local swimming pool. This was quickly followed by the shock that my own baby sister—freshly pink and implacable—was one of those being tossed. Of course, all this was done under the fretful gaze of my mother, who, like the other mothers, would stand in the waist-deep water while the fathers stooped at poolside and gently dropped their infant children. After the hush there would be a grand, syncopated splash and then the mad scramble of baby retrieval in the foam.

My girlfriends and I, shapeless bodies hidden under our bikinis, watched this in silence from the springboards at the other end of the pool, stupefied. We had grown up with the conviction—burned into consciousness by our parents—that water, although great fun, presented countless enticements to death. And so we lived with ironclad parental injunctions, veritable commandments of swimming: the thirty-minute post-lunch wait, the no-spitting-water rule, the zero-tolerance policy on horseplay. We had water wings and flutter boards clamped to us and were subjected to swimming lessons so unremitting and arduous that it should have alerted child welfare authorities. Whenever fatigue or faltering technique caused us to begin to sink, our swim coaches would exhort us with the universal command intended to forestall drowning: *kick*, they screamed. We kicked a lot. So the change in our parents' attitudes— almost more than the act of throwing babies into the pool—caught us completely by surprise; I stood on the springboard, gape-mouthed. Anything was possible.

Soon after that, I remember seeing this sort of activity shown repeatedly on television. Footage from underwater cameras captured the crystalline splash of countless babies like my sister. The infants were always shown paddling through clear blue water, looking infinitely pleased and confident, like astronauts on a spacewalk. This was the new way to learn to swim. Humans were natural swimmers, it was argued; lessons and graphic warnings only generated unnecessary fear, estranging us from our natural, amphibian tendencies. And so the flinging began.

My mother now downplays her participation in the baby-flinging method of swim training that gripped the nation in those days, although when it's mentioned, like now when I bring it up in the spirit of communal nostalgia, she defends the action or, more precisely, the motivation behind it.

"It made your sister a great swimmer," she says.

Janet lifts her head enough that we can all register the basset-hound arch of her eyebrow.

"Well, you *are*," she continues, always retaining the right to be offended by the incredulity of her daughters.

My mother gets up to clear away the emptied tea cups and the plate with two remaining shortbread cookies, clearly performing the act with more vigour than is necessary. An undisguised clattering in the sink, the audible snap of a dish towel.

"You *had* to mention it," Janet drones, not looking up from the curling pieces of paper in front of her.

I close my eyes. From outside my kitchen window the reports of crickets rise, almost drowned out by the adenoidal hiss of the baby monitor. The cupboard door claps closed in punctuation. A breeze sifts through the rooms on the first floor, gently eddying doors on their hinges. I imagine the air pouring upstairs like an ocean current, brushing my sleeping son's hand, rippling under the crib that holds my daughter. Tonight the whole house feels like a giant animal taking short skimming breaths. My sister shifts to get comfortable under her growing stomach. She exhales after this manoeuvre, the effort almost sufficient to create a sigh. My mother, hurt feelings forgotten, returns to the table. When I open my eyes, my mother and sister are sitting there just as I've imagined, which shocks and delights me.

My sister stares intently at the image in front of her, disengaging only to shuffle the papers and view the next. A pointillist work in black and white clusters that form a line or a swirl that from a distance could represent the gathering winds of a hurricane. But on the paper that has her name on its corner she swears that she can make out the curve of a human forehead, tracing it with her forefinger. In another, a heart is caught between its hummingbird beats. My favourite is one where out of complete visual chaos a perfect gloved hand of delicate bone emerges, as though pressed up against a pane of glass.

"They don't tell you the sex anymore, do they?" I say.

"Lawsuits," Janet replies. "People paint the baby's room pink, buy dresses, and choose girls' names, all based on the ultrasound and ... whoops."

"Still, that's a lovely surprise," my mother says, "a little penis." She pauses after saying *penis*, as though luxuriating in the reticent thrill. Grandchildren have made it safe for her to say the word in company.

When I was pregnant with my first I was as excited and curious as anyone, but those books designed to tell you what to expect during pregnancy seemed vague or focused on issues like properly decorating the baby's room; so instead I bought an embryology textbook from the university bookstore and read about what was happening inside me. The diagrams showed how the cells moved in an orderly way to form a plate that pinched and folded into a tube. In this way a brain was assembled, its surface corrugating, connections made that would eventually be another universe. Within weeks a shrimp-shaped mass had budded limbs and taken on a human form, cells streaming in every direction, bringing a body into existence. It was as though I could hear the activity humming inside me. Janet's husband, Bob, who's an anaesthesiologist, once found me reading the book and hovered silently over my shoulder. He said nothing, but I knew what he was thinking. He was right I suppose; it did keep me awake nights, thinking about the complexity of the whole thing, the journeys that had to be completed. All those contingencies. When my son was born, fantastically normal, I put the book away. For my second it stayed on the shelf.

The monitor crackles, relaying the stirrings of my daughter down to us. We look at each other, all of us silent for a moment, waiting for her voice to call out for me, but nothing comes. Janet has finished studying the last of her ultrasound pictures. It shows the clearest image of her unborn child floating in a sea of deepest, amniotic black. She's happy, of course, but she also has that other look, an extra furrow that I've worn and that I'm certain my mother knows as well. For anyone looking in at us through the window of this suburban house I suppose we three must appear to be a picture of contentedness, even self-satisfaction. But my sister's face shows more than that. She hears the hum. Yes, it's different here at the table, more complicated. I just sit beside her, thinking of what I can say to help, but no words seem to do. Besides, in a moment a kick will come without anyone's urging.

J.R. Carpenter

Precipice

A habitual stomach-sleeper, she dreams of falling. Face down, the falling is more like flying; she never hits the ground. Often in her dreams of falling there is a precipice: a clearly defined line before which, perhaps for acres on end, grow grassy, sloping fields of thistle, pock-marked by dry caked dung. And after? Arriving at the precipice all fields and fences end abruptly and fall away. Forty feet below, there lies a beach of stones; a scree face, driftwood and bones; a vague sense of bottom. And beyond: an inordinate amount of ocean.

Her husband is an early riser. Lately he takes no joy in this, though. He has not been sleeping well. He lies awake for hours, as still as possible so as not to disturb her. He watches her; she sleeps on her stomach with her arms tucked neatly by her sides. She sleeps like a superhero, he thinks, like she is flying through the sky. He takes the first hint of dawn as permission to slip out of bed.

For all the hiss and stickiness of this humid summer, the days are not quite hot. There is no breeze coming up from the ocean this year—only a fine salt mist insisting on seeping into everything, staining his soon-to-be hay. The combine waits impassively, lurking with the bailer in the dusty, sagging barn. It would not rain, not when he needed it to. Now that haying season is nearing, he fears it will rain torrentially and spoil his beleaguered bails before he can get them under cover. So far he has hidden these worries from his wife.

The dream of the precipice begins with driving: there is a grey cracked road, and God knows who-all crowded into a rusted, limping car. After the driving she walks and walks. Even asleep, she is tired from it. The walking is framed by a false horizon. The fields are humid, dull and rough—not meadows at all. There are mosquitoes, and the land is in debt. Little by lots by little, the edge edges closer, egged on by the overzealous ocean and the weak, capricious cliff. The edge of the earth is a tangible thing when the edge of your farm is being eaten away by erosion, by inches each and every year. When the end is near, she drops to the ground. The sensation of falling/not-falling becomes precise. Lying on her stomach she pulls herself forward by her elbows towards the precipice, arms twitching by her sides in her sleep.

He was glad when his wife's family came to visit; it was lonely for her, living way out here. She was like them, and he was not. Although she never said a word about it, he knew she missed the mass of them: the noise and strength of their talents and charms. They arrived unannounced along with a thunderstorm early in August. "Surprise!" her mother exclaimed, the first one out of the cramped car. She hugged her daughter while an assortment of younger siblings and cousins tumbled out onto the gravel driveway. "We just happened to be in the neighbourhood, you know, darling, driving around out here on the edge of the earth."

During their visit, his wife's youngest brother asked him, "How many cows do you have?" He had to think about it, but he didn't want to. There wasn't going to be enough hay to feed the dairy heard this season; there was no money to buy any more. Sooner or later he was going to have to cut his losses. Livestock prices were falling like bricks. He took a walk that morning after milking. He took his young brother-in-law out for a tour of the fodder and the barn.

She watched the worry gather up behind his placid brow, invisible like the salt in the air, deceptive like the August thunder that brought no rain. "I don't mind a little bit of ruin," she said. "It doesn't matter. The farm is shrinking anyway. So what? We'll sell some cattle in the fall. You know I like the auctions ... When we're in town remind me, I'd like to give Peggy a call."

It had been quite some time since he had walked out to the furthest limit of his farm, out to where the field fell into the ocean. He had accepted the erosion as a sad fact, a reminder of his inexperience. When the precipice loomed near, he dropped to the ground. Wary of the overhang, he pulled himself forward on his stomach by his elbows towards the edge of the pasture. He couldn't face not knowing. How could his wife stand it? She worked all day and slept all night. She never looked their precariousness straight in the eye.

She lies on her stomach on her bed in her sleep in her dream on the edge of a field that juts out into a nothingness. Everyone knows about the overhang. There is an absence of soil beneath the sod, a fine line between her and falling to a rock-sharp and salt-watery grave. She lies low and spreads her weight out as evenly as possible. "What if the lemmings come?" she thinks suddenly, and in her sleep her sleepless husband hears her laugh. If, just about now, a mass of lemmings—driven mad by overpopulation—were rushing hell-bent for her particular edge of the earth, perhaps the scales would tip. Perhaps the overhang would give way as a thousand, thousand tiny claws and tails raced across her back. Pushing her over the precipice, their bitty little bodies would do nothing to break her fall.

ELISE MOSER

Malke's Baby

They are preparing to leave. The jewellery has been sold, even the wedding ring and the tiny pearl earrings that studded the baby's ears. It is frightening to flee; it has become even more frightening to stay. Above all, the baby must not grow up in this grey constriction, never taking a full breath of sweet air into her pink lungs, her eyes never learning to see farther than the closest wall. It is for her that they are taking this risk.

All must appear as normal from the outside. The curtains, threadbare but clean, hang in the windows undisturbed. The enamelled vase, tall with wildflowers, visible before the drapery. Malke put fresh flowers there yesterday morning, collected from beside the railroad tracks.

This is nerve-wracking. They thought it was hard living in this slowly shrinking bell jar, always waiting for a stray word or an accidental movement to trigger brutal fate. But this is much harder. Even as they stew in agony for fear their furtive preparations will be discovered, their napes still prickle at the possibilities of ordinary life: arrest, beating, death. Malke wraps the baby in a clean flannel blanket, washed in rusty water, hung to dry over the stove burning the legs of a scuffed endtable. Now the ashes lie cold, and the child's tiny hands are like small, animate curls of ice.

Malke holds the baby to her chest and rubs the small back. Her own hands will never be warm; she hasn't had enough food for too long. But the baby should not suffer. Malke feels an awful weight of guilt—sometimes it squeezes her lungs so hard she can barely breathe—for bringing the child forth into this terrible world. But it is the only world there is, the only one she had to offer. Now she will gamble everything to bring the child farther, out of death and misery.

She imagines the baby lying red-cheeked in sunlight, fat and happy, reaching for her own toes.

There is a thump outside, and Malke's stomach burns, her breath caught in her throat. They are perfectly still, listening with their entire bodies. Whoever it was moves away. Exhale. Malke sees she has been clutching the baby's wrist so hard it has turned briefly white. Her stomach burns again. Her stomach burns all the time. The young husband stands by the back door, a sack half-filled with essentials slung ready across his shoulder. The adults have no clothes left, there is no food; their essentials are blankets and diapers for the baby, and one tiny, beautifully embroidered dress made by the hands of Malke's mother, now, like almost everyone, dead.

Malke looks around the small, cold room. The furniture has all been burned for warmth except the very last piece, big and heavy and hard to chop apart: a wardrobe. The pride of Malke's mother's bedroom set. Open the inlaid cherry wood doors, and there is room to hang clothes, although nothing hangs there now. There are two wide drawers, once filled with nightgowns, handkerchiefs, linens. Now empty, too, except the soft towel in the bottom drawer, laid there to receive the baby in case of a raid. With the heavy doors closed, no-one would hear her.

The man who delivers milk to the barracks has taken the young husband's gold watch, given him by his father upon his marriage. In return, the dairy farmer will detour past their alleyway at dawn, when his wagon holds only empty milk cans. He will signal them by whistling a love song. The plan is that he will quickly cover Malke, her husband, and the baby with straw and push the empty milk cans around them, and then drive them out into the countryside, where another smuggler will meet them and take them farther.

Malke warms the baby's bottle of water with the last crumbs of sugar dissolved in it, by putting it under her arm and wishing. The little girl is pushing her limbs out at the world, unaware that it despises her; her wet red bud of a mouth purses, searching for the nipple which, now that Malke is empty of milk, must be on the end of a bottle of water. At least it will fill her stomach. While the baby sucks, Malke chews her own shredded fingernails. The iron taste of her own blood is comforting, it has become so familiar. The night has been long, but it is coming to an end. Malke strains her ears for the sound of the farmer's whistling.

Instead, the empty stillness of the dark room is ruptured by the sudden racket of boots on the cobblestones outside. They hear the shouts ringing through the street and the pounding on doors. Malke's heart flies up, frantically trying to escape through her mouth, but it is blocked by her involuntary cry. Immediately, she and the young husband snap into their much-practiced raid drill. Automatically, Malke gently but quickly deposits the baby in the drawer of the wardrobe. Tears running down her face, she kisses the small forehead. As she closes the drawer she sees the baby placidly sucking one of her own tiny dear fingers; her eyes are half-closed, the sugar in her belly soothing her to sleep. Malke closes the heavy wardrobe doors, blessing them: her baby will not be swung by the feet, her tiny skull smashed against the stone wall. God willing.

Her hand at her own throat, Malke runs to the back door with her husband. They crack it open and slip, hunched, just outside, and then they hear shouting behind them, and the sickening impact as the front door of their room splinters. Startled like rabbits, they are running, heads bent, through the damp passage between crumbling walls. As they run, they hear, at the mouth of the alleyway, the urgent but tuneful whistling of the farmer's song. Panicked, they leap into the wagon, between the dull and dented milk cans.

The shouting of soldiers and the crackling of gunshots have faded behind them; they have lain under the heaps of straw, their hearts beating so hard they have not been able to think of anything but that wild thudding, the hissing of breath. The wagon is rattling away on the rutted road leading from the sad city into the surrounding countryside when Malke's heart bursts in her; she rises, wailing, festooned with straw like some anguished barn ghost. She leaps for the empty space beyond the end of the wagon bed; it is all the young husband can do to hold her ankles, to keep her from throwing herself into the road and running back to the city. She would never arrive, and they would all be condemned—the farmer, too. The husband crushes her against his chest, his heart roiling; she tears the flesh of her face with her fingers.

DEBORAH OSTROVSKY

As Amadoras

*It is necessary to "command" a fingerboard, to wield a cello bow with
authority. Without what we call mastery, the physical resistance of the
instrument together with the awkwardness to which all conscious endeavour
is prone would reduce our margin of freedom—the scope of our eloquence—
to zero.*

> – Marcus Adeney, *Tomorrow's Cellist: Exploring the Basis
>   of Artistry*, 1984

Sintra Goldson breathed deeply and exited the foyer of the conservatory. *Ah, Freedom. No mastery, but freedom*, she thought as she
wrapped her knuckles across the back of her cello case three times.
This was her daily ritual while descending the conservatory's front
steps, when returning home after so many lessons. Today, she would
take a detour and walk past the harbour.

Her name had not been on the orchestra list. Her sisters, Audrée,
Tosca, and Hinda, the Goldson daughters—that triumvirate of
talent—were there. They were assigned principal chairs indicated
by gold stars pinned next to their names on the dilapidated conservatory corkboard. Tosca, *wunderkind*, concertmistress; Hinda,
principal second violin; Audrée, principal viola. But Sintra,
violoncello, the eldest ... waiting list.

Sintra's audition had been horrible. She was so nervous that she
had excused herself to go to the bathroom in the middle of the *Lalo
Concerto*. What was considered a perfunctory exercise to secure places
each year for her sisters had almost caused Sintra's bladder to empty
itself like the weakened membrane of a balloon.

Her talent had always fallen short of an unnamed something.
As she walked down the tree-lined street she recalled what her mother,

Esther, once told her. "Sintra," she had said, "you have impeccable musical syntax, but there is ... something. Being musical is a thing one *is*; it cannot be feigned. Music is sacred, and the profane cannot parade itself as saintly if it feels apathetic about the urgency embedded in a phrase, or fainthearted at the sight of a *crescendo*."

Sintra had no real explanation for her musical shortcomings. Unlike her sisters, she had been conceived in an era of musical insecurity. Her parents had not planned her. Nor had they planned to be together. Theo and Esther had been talented but penniless musicians, both violinists, playing every chamber-music festival across Southern Europe. They were married to other musicians and had first met during a festival in the Portuguese city of her namesake, Sintra. As they explained to the girls years later, they'd started sleeping together rather by accident.

"Everything precious starts with hard work, improvisation, and lightness," Esther told them with a sultry laugh. "Your father and I worked hard to become musicians. Falling in love was easy."

"Nor was it all that difficult," Theo added, "to get out of our first marriages when the real *magnum opus* lay before us."

As she walked towards the city quays, Sintra tried to remember the scandalous details of her parents' courtship. Esther suspected her pregnancy with Sintra while in Lisbon, hiding away from both her husband and her lover in a grotty *pensão*, disgraced as she was by the salacious rumours among other musicians about their affair. News spread like wildfire of their secret "rehearsals." They made love after midnight, with Esther's body pinned up against the *alentejo*-tiled walls in the courtyards of the Sintra castle gardens; at other times, underneath the scaffolding of the empty orchestral stage.

In Lisbon, Sintra's mother noticed changes in her body. She developed cravings for sweets, custards, and pastries. Her breasts became heavy. She walked the labyrinthine cobblestone streets, her violin strapped around her like a heavy sash, hands cupped over her mouth because of nausea. Deep-fried shellfish wafted in odorous plumes from every corner *restaurante*. Eventually Theo found her, and he phoned his wife Cynthia to tell her he was leaving. Esther made a similar call to her husband that night, with what remained of their phone card. They married several months after Sintra's birth, following messy divorces that somehow left them unscathed.

Sintra hated her name, the city of her parents' marital transgressions, the site of their unrelenting spontaneity. Nor was she fond of the way they told their courtship story with such insouciance. It was unbearable how Esther jumped at the chance to tell it at parties, weddings.

Sintra's lack of talent: Esther thought it was possibly the result of delivery by caesarean section. The surgical birth, perhaps, denied Sintra musicality inspired by passage through the birth canal. Luckily, the obstetrician was able to make a low uterine incision. Tosca, Audrée, and Hinda arrived without the interference of scalpels like those used to yank their older sister out of their mother's belly, robbing Sintra of perfect pitch and intonation. Consequently, Sintra's sisters floated on the confidence of their uncanny talents, their august and sensual musicality. They were only teenagers, but they looked like Raphaelite nymphs, ageless girl-women with long auburn ringlets that had an unkempt charm. Sintra, aged seventeen, was the odd one out. The cello was physically at odds with her tiny boylike frame, her bony wrists buckling with every bowstroke. Everything about the cello's weightiness annoyed her, its lugubrious whining, its frivolous sadness. Her cello bellowed endlessly, making harsh crunches when her bow changed direction. Sintra knew the instrument's ugly potential, its grunts, and the highly unromantic rituals of practicing. But then—there were moments: moments when the cello's beauty was so astonishing that she felt a sharp pain, a shudder of sadness and rage all mixed into one.

As she walked closer to the pier, Sintra remembered her family's trip to Portugal for the same festival where her parents had first met. The conductor that year, João Silva, was so enchanted by the girls that he offered them a musical gift: a string quartet for children he had composed called *As Amadoras*—"The Amateurs." The piece was a parody, a spoof on musical themes——Brahms, Shostakovich, Mozart—mimicking a cacophony of sounds made by an untalented group of players. As the girls performed it for the first time, the adults around them burst into peals of laughter. They climbed up tuneless scales in clumsy pentatonic harmonies, making a mockery of passages from famous works. *As Amadoras*, said João Silva, is entertaining; but it should be played as a reminder that being a musician is not a choice, but a calling. To be a musician is to go out there, into the world, bravely, even when the sounds we create seem ridiculous.

Everyone thought *As Amadoras* was marvelous. Sintra thought it was cruel. *We have no right,* she thought, *to mock the unenviable plight of the less gifted.*

As Sintra finally approached the end of the pier, she remembered passages her father once read to her from a well-known cellist's memoirs.

You and your cello are the same organism, the same tissue and fluids. Do not command your cello; let it be a part of you, as the air you breathe. Mastery comes with practice, but also listening. Your cello complains loudly when you do not play like you should. As you listen, you and your cello will become each other's masters.

Sintra foisted her cello case up unto her shoulder until it was perched against her head like a giant water jug. Standing on the pier's edge, she let the cello case slide off her shoulder. She watched as it plunged into the water and then floated along the waves like a bobbing coffin. The neck of the instrument lifted and turned from side to side like an arrowhead.

She wondered where the cello would go, now that she was free.

Weathering the Storm

Melanie wanted to be transformed by the storm that raged on Ste-Catherine, lulled by the force of Mother Nature's white ferocity, and mesmerized by the chaos of crawling traffic and slip-sliding pedestrians on Montreal's busiest shopping street. Yet, the mix of howling wind and angry horns only aggravated the thumping baseline resonating down from above to her empty store.

The ruling was clear, for the love of God: no loud music until the store closed. Melanie stared at the ceiling and willed it to stop. *Call Marlow*, but she knew his litany by heart: *It's not my problem. You'll have to work it out with him. He pays his rent.* Frustrated, she debated storming up and making a scene in *the club*. She was near the point where she didn't care: Melanie's Mothers & Maternity, MMM, no longer gave her the same satisfaction.

As she started to close her cash, Melanie longed for the Caplans. An old Jewish couple who'd made women's clothes in the loft above for nearly forty years. They had patiently taught her the skill of purchasing clothes, and, once, they had given her the humbling gift of a no-questions-asked, interest-free short-term loan when she experienced cash-flow problems in her fourth year. But, by MMM's sixth anniversary, super-discount chains and cheap-labour imports forced the Caplans out of business.

The loft remained empty for nearly a year. Then demolition crews appeared one day and started smashing. She asked them what they were doing, but her questions fell on deaf ears. She phoned Marlow, and he didn't return her calls. When the construction crews started banging, rattling her store along with browsing customers, she went upstairs. She couldn't find the elusive proprietor—even today, she still didn't know what he looked like. Then, the gaudy picture went up with:

SEX FULL CONTACT SEX

Only then did she understand the elusive behaviour. Ironically, business went up, but that didn't change the principle of the matter. Just as the court case hadn't really changed anything. The rhythmic thumping incensed her. *That's it, I've had enough!*

A customer walked in. *Great.* Snow and wind gusted in, making the maternity dresses on the racks billow with life. One glance, and Melanie knew the woman had chosen the wrong door.

"Can I help you?" But Melanie's tone screamed, *You don't belong here.*

"I ... no ... I ... just wanted to look. I—"

"You work—" Melanie's eyes shifted towards the ceiling and back again.

"Yes," the woman said defiantly. At the same moment, a chill chased Melanie's spine: she knew those olive-green eyes. Eyes that had cut her to pieces three years ago. Eyes that bled a mix of sadness, anger, and despair: her daughter's eyes. The woman turned to leave; Melanie verged on panic.

"I'm sorry. It's the thumping from above," Melanie pleaded and pointed to her head.

"Migraine."

The woman hesitated.

"What's your name?" Melanie asked quickly.

"Athena," she said, the edges softening a little.

"The name of a Greek goddess—"

"Born from the head of Zeus," Athena injected sardonically, her mouth smiling, her eyes not. Melanie frowned: a *stripper* who knew Greek mythology?

The windows rattled, and both women watched the storm's intensity.

With it, the nightmare fight strobed in Melanie's memories.

Always your needs, always your wants. No wonder Dad left you!

And the impossible slap. The one Melanie could never take back.

Athena's hand gingerly caressed the baby clothes on the specials rack.

"Anything in particular you're looking for?" Melanie asked. She moved from behind the counter, closer to where Athena stood. The gentle scent of *Femme* tickled Melanie's nose.

"A friend ... was going to have a baby. And lost it."

"That's too bad. A miscarriage?" Melanie asked, and Athena's eyes shifted.

"No. Well, yes. It's complicated," Athena said, and Melanie understood the white lie.

"I've always wanted to come in and look. You didn't seem busy..."

"I'm glad you did," Melanie said, smiling. Athena nodded, her strained smile like the sun trying to penetrate through an iffy day. Melanie wanted to touch her, but Athena moved to browse through the clothes on another maternity rack.

"You have my daughter's eyes." *Jesus, why did I say that!*

"How old is she?" Athena asked, now touching baby tops.

"Twenty-three."

"That's my age!" Athena blurted, her eyes penetrating; Melanie took a reflexive step back.

"What's her name?" Athena asked quietly, controlled.

"Alexandria."

Athena opened her mouth. Changed her mind. Closed it. She moved to another baby-ensemble rack, then asked, "What does she do?"

"She's ... a poet." Melanie didn't add: *Okanagan fruit picker, and welfare recipient the rest of the year.*

"Where?"

"In Vancouver," Melanie said, uneasy. Then it dawned on her: she'd been following Athena too closely. Athena stopped browsing and studied her. *Those eyes.* Melanie knew that her makeup could only hide so many lines.

"I was in Vancouver once. Lots of rain. But at least they don't get this."

Both women looked outside. The snow, big-fluffy cotton balls now, swirled about gently.

"It is beautiful, though. At least we get four seasons and not just two."

Athena didn't comment; she renewed her browsing. Then she stopped, pursed her lips, and frowned. "The music really is loud, isn't it."

"I was going to go up and—"

"That's not a good idea—for you, I mean. I'll talk to Hertsy—I mean, Mr. Hertz. I know how to ... talk to him. Besides, women should have peace and quiet in here."

She wanted to ask about *Hertsy*, but Athena moved, and the moment evaporated.

"It's going to be quiet tonight. With the storm and Christmas. People buying presents for—" Athena let her words die, looking, but no longer seeing the fabric or the material she slowly released.

"Yes," Melanie said, averting her eyes to the activity outside.

"Well, I have to get to work. It was nice meeting you," Athena extended her hand. Melanie reciprocated. She was surprised by Athena's warmth and firm grip.

"It was nice of you to drop by. Come in anytime."

"Alright, thank you. I'd say the same ... but ... well—"

"That's alright." Melanie marveled at Athena's beautiful white teeth. The cloud cover broke—her eyes smiled, for a moment. Then both women released their hold, reluctantly. Athena's high heels click-clicked away, awkwardly. At the door, she turned before she pushed through. She gave Melanie a small wave. Melanie smiled and waved back. A weak draft of snow pushed through as Athena opened the door. She made a graceful U-turn and disappeared.

Melanie felt something, an ache she couldn't rationalize. Her hand danced through baby racks and then maternity racks and then back again. She wandered about the store and folded and refolded shirts and sweaters and pullovers and skirts and wraparounds and bras and...

Melanie stopped. She felt a change, a presence. She looked outside: snowflakes parachuted gently, cars and people inched along a little faster. Then it dawned on her: the thumping, the boom-boom-boom, had stopped. Athena had convinced Mr. Hertz to lower the volume, the pressure.

Thank you.

She found herself behind the counter, behind the phone. *How did I get here?*

Salt in her mouth, the phone beckoned her. Alexandria's number: 604-by heart.

Melanie's whole body started to thump—boom, boom, boom.

Bats

I wait with the engine off, till the porch light goes on and the moths start stabbing into the light with their wings. As Lina makes her way to the truck, I notice her hair is a puffed up at the crown of her head, as if she's been sleeping on it all day.

"How's the baby?" I ask, turning onto the highway, as she lights one of my cigarettes.

"Alright. Cranky as hell though."

She pulls the rear-view down and smoothes her eyes with her fingers.

"How's Lloyd doing?"

"Uh, good. He's got a new contract, so he's pretty tired. Money's good though."

I used to do roofing with Lloyd until my shoulder got dislocated. I couldn't really keep up with Lloyd, though he was too nice to say anything.

When we get to the shack, I leave the high beams on for a second so we can decide how to plod our way through the spider webs. Then I follow Lina into the rotted house and don't turn on my flashlight till we're inside.

"You do the left."

"Sure thing," I say, waving the flashlight to the top left corner, where, under a wet broken beam, a group of twenty or so bats sway.

They got married young. Too young, some thought. Lina received a biology scholarship in the city after high school but said she'd defer it until after the wedding. I was best man. I don't remember much of the reception, though everybody said I made a really funny speech. Lloyd had saved enough from roofing part-time to take Lina to

Acapulco for their honeymoon. But I knew Lina wanted to go somewhere less touristy, like Portugal or Cuba.

I'd engaged Lina's father in a conversation so that I wouldn't have to talk to them or look at them too long when they walked across the dance floor to say their goodbyes. As they came towards us, I tried to shake off the high-frequency pitch that throbbed through my skull. The world, it seemed to me, had been reduced to a wild, spinning, place. The only person I could focus on was Lina; I smiled at her and imagined her eyes were desperate, that they locked on mine. Then, with one eye shut, I shook Lloyd's hand and toasted them off.

But I do remember my hangover the next day and how I had to drive seven hours back to the city as the image of my best friend's wife's back, tanning in the Mexican sun, sprawled across the winter highway as I drank my fifth coffee. Her smell: sharp sweat, mixed with pineapple and talc, still with me. No matter how many cigarettes I smoked.

Sometimes they swoop down, waking up mid-drop.

"Ugly, little, blind bats," Lina whispers, covering her mouth. Their musty smell is almost overwhelming.

"How many did you get?"

"Seventy-three."

She does some quick mental calculations and smiles.

"Their breeding is up!"

"Let's get in the car. It's getting cold."

When we get back to Lina's, Lloyd is up with the baby, who is bundled in her car seat, on the kitchen counter.

Lloyd has that glow of a man who's been drinking alone for a couple of hours. He gives Lina a crazy grin before catching her up in a bear hug. The baby coos at the two of them as Lloyd plucks another two beers from the fridge and hands me one. Lina opens the fridge and gathers four beers against her chest quickly, as if she fears someone will stop her.

"We're going to the boathouse. Dan's going to play me some songs on his guitar."

"Okay. How're the bats?"

"Busy."

I sit at the back of the boathouse, close to the candle, because one of the hardest things in the world is playing guitar in the dark.

I start plucking out different tunes, trying to think of a song to play for Lina that will wipe the distracted look from her face.

"Hey, wake up, Dan." Lina flicks water on me. She laughs uncontrollably, stupidly. I realize that she's kind of drunk.

"You okay?"

"Yeah. I didn't eat much today, beer went straight to my head."

"No kidding. So, I think I'll head home, pick the truck up in the morning."

"Don't. Not yet. Stay for a minute."

"Sure thing," I say, thinking of the beaten path behind the boathouse to my trailer. How it takes exactly sixteen and a half minutes to walk to the trailer at night, less in the morning. How the path runs parallel to the river and how, if I start walking now, I will be seeing the same curve of water Lina will in a minute.

"You got to do me a favour."

"What's that?" I say, in a friendly way.

She takes my hand while looking over her shoulder at the house.

"What is it?"

She holds my hand so tightly the bones in her palms crush my knuckles. With her free hand, she pulls up her layers of shirts. She molds a fist of my hand and places it high, right under her ribs, and then moves it back, like a careful mime, making a slow pendulum of my arm.

"I'm late, Dan, like two months late." Her voice is suddenly very sober.

"I think this is something you should talk about with Lloyd, really." I finger my pocket, looking for a stray cigarette. In the light of the match, I close my eyes and concentrate on the orange colour of the flame behind my lids. Then I imagine the narrow trail, the cool dark earth, below me.

"Please, Dan, it's awful, I know, but it's easier, so much easier..."

"For who?" I snap, pacing up and down the creaking floorboards. As the smoke inundates my lungs I wait for the feeling of it entering my blood, my hands, until I get that certainty of time being slower, heavier.

She turns her back to me, sways slightly, and asks: "What do you think of when you look at the river Dan?"

"Nothing, I don't think about anyone. What do you think of?"

"I think of diving upstream, like a salmon, you know, swimming against it, to that big salmon Mecca..."

"Don't be dramatic, hey, get away from the edge." I hook my arm through hers and pull her back a bit.

"Please, Dan." And I see us, arching into the water, like bent arrows, like half-asleep bats, soaring for a second, straight down into the river.

"This is crazy. I can't punch you, Lina. I can't."

She folds into me, sobbing. I close my eyes again and see the path before me, only a few steps away now. I see the river next to her shoulder heaving a stray branch along. I think of the word *womb*. I say it over and over silently, moving only my lips. It makes me feel safe, hearing it transform itself with repetition: *womb, room, swoon, groom, june* ... I smell the pine, the mosquito repellent in Lina's hair, the warm yeasty smell of beer coming from her mouth, and I hold her to me.

MATTHEW ANDERSON

Marathon of Hope

It was the Marathon of Hope weekend when Virgil met his first dead person. He had been looking forward all week to the Saturday-night rerun of Seinfeld's final three episodes; had told his friends that he couldn't go out—he'd be busy that evening. He'd even bought some microwave popcorn and a six-pack of beer for his tiny apartment fridge. Although he knew he would only have two, buying six like that for no other reason than staying home alone made him feel like it was a special occasion.

At ten minutes to nine, everything was ready: pillow, remote, popcorn, beer. When the television came on, however, what Virgil saw was the seniors of the local Lions Club, dressed in their gold and burgundy sashes, singing "K-K-K-Katie" while volunteers—he recognized one of the ladies from church—held up signs announcing *$29,346 raised so far.*

It was the "so far" that sealed it. "Okay. Alright," he told himself, "still a few minutes to go." But he knew. A 72-hour fundraising marathon was not going to take an hour off to show a series ender, not when the lineup included the baton-twirling glee club The Beaverettes from the local junior high and the special presentation of $3000 by a grinning member of the Chamber of Commerce decked out in an electric-blue baseball cap with a logo proclaiming *Busy Beaver Business Booster.*

When the phone rang, he answered it.

"Is this the student minister?"

"The vicar, yes. Can I help you?"

"Do you know where the pastor is?"

"Sorry. Did you try calling him at home?"

"He's not there."

"Then I guess I don't. He didn't say anything to me. There's nothing on at the church. Far as I know."

"We need someone down here."

"Here?"

"At the hospital. Right now. My dad is dying."

At the hospital he didn't wait for the elevators but took the stairs two at a time to the third floor and was pointed to the darkened room. He slowed at the door, afraid he might accidentally walk up to the wrong bed.

Waking up in a chronic care ward to find a priest—even a vicar—hovering over you can be a shock. Virgil had already seen how, on visiting days at the hospital, certain patients would shy away from his black shirt and Bible, as if somehow he were not the comforter of the sick but the herald of ill tidings.

Tonight there was no danger of mistaking the patient. A small lamp burned beside only one of the beds in the large public ward, while the curtains were drawn around the other five. A knot of people hunched over the old man lying there. His face was grizzled and shrunk in, like a piece of hairy dried fruit. There was a whistling sound, and it took Virgil a moment to realize that it was coming not from the heating system but from the old man. It sounded vaguely automobile-like, as if he were a poorly tuned car engine heard from a distance, failing in its struggle to keep idling on a cold day.

The family parted to allow him access to the bed. The railing was up. Its chrome felt cool against his brand-new clerical garb as he leaned over to look at the old man.

They had no idea, of course, that he had never done this before. Whatever you do, do it slowly, he told himself. The old man's eyes were closed.

For a while Virgil just stood there, in that small circle of warm light, looking over the bed. It felt to him so like a cocoon. Or maybe a place of worship, the far-off murmurs of the nurses at their station like prayers over the sombre ostinato of another patient snoring lightly somewhere in that dry darkness.

"He was awake yesterday afternoon." A balding man now standing at Virgil's right elbow broke his reverie. The man was a fuller, taller version of the patient. The son.

"Has he been—?" Virgil let the question drop, hoping they would fill it in as needed.

"In a coma since then," finished another, perhaps a daughter.

Virgil took the service book in one hand, and then the old man's hand in his other. It was a calloused hand, a farmer's hand, and he had expected it to be limp, but even in a coma the old man grasped and held on. Until that moment Virgil hadn't really thought of the body in the bed as a real person. As the old man's grip tightened, Virgil felt his neck shudder, and then his back, right down between his shoulder blades.

With his right hand now trapped, Virgil managed with his left to brace the book against his chest and flip open awkwardly the page marked "Rites for Death and Dying." He read a psalm and a prayer, and then stopped, to see how things felt. That was appropriate, he judged, but it didn't feel like quite enough. He read another text, this time from the New Testament, and then another prayer. Since he felt more comfortable now and the family seemed in no hurry, he continued. Somewhere between that moment and his reading of the twenty-third psalm, he realized that the whistling had stopped, the grip gone soft.

Around him, the family was quiet, except for the sobbing of one of the granddaughters. Virgil realized he had probably been the last to know that the man had died.

Everyone now seemed to be waiting for him to say or do something. He put down his book, took the hand he had been holding, and folded it over the stiff blue cotton of the hospital gown on the old man's chest. The hand stayed in place only a few seconds, then started to slide down, and almost fell off the bed before he caught it. Again Virgil stood a moment, unsure of what to do. He bent the old man's arm at the elbow slightly and was able to balance the weight of the arm on the old man's chest, partly by inserting the hand, Napoleon-like, into the front of the hospital gown. Finally Virgil held his own right hand, finally liberated, in the blessing position.

"Let light perpetual shine upon him. In the name of the Father, and of the Son—" he made the sign of the cross over the grizzled white face "—and of the Holy Spirit."

Virgil paused, letting the silence build.

"Amen," said the son, the others joining in before Virgil could finish.

Virgil was up until three-thirty that morning, watching the Cub Car Rally Finals, a Four-H Farm Club presentation on proper techniques for cattle vaccination, and a group of Highland Dancers. By the time he had finished all the beer, a little girl, aged eight, dressed in a purple crushed velvet dress was singing "Somewhere over the Rainbow" in a quavering voice that for some reason made him cry.

Brent Laughren

The Tin Ceiling

He woke up staring at the old tin ceiling in the bedroom—a sight which had greeted his parents every morning of their married life and the first thing he, himself, must have seen having been born in this very same bed. His wife had wanted to paint the bedroom when they'd taken over the homestead, but he'd insisted it remain as it was with the flecks of green and yellow showing through the white paint.

His father had wanted to die in this bed, or at least in his own home, but that hadn't happened. The cancer had been aggressive and spread so rapidly he never got to go home. Instead, he died in hospital hooked to tubes with a machine doing his breathing for him—a man who had never before set foot in a hospital. He only got out once—a Sunday afternoon for a drive. "The morphine drip will keep him comfortable," the nurse had said, "but don't keep him out too long because he'll tire quickly."

He'd taken his father to the back side of the old sugar bush because he was afraid the old man would get too agitated if they went by the homestead on the other side. It was a quiet afternoon, and the maple trees were ablaze with colour. He parked by the side of the road in the sunlight so his father would feel warmer, but the sun was pretty weak. Here, one fall afternoon when they were out hunting partridge, his father had told him that young lovers used to come by horse and buggy. In fact, in an unusual burst of candour, his father had said it was right here one afternoon in late May, under a wild apple tree in full blossom, that he'd proposed to his future wife.

They sat in silence under that same tree for about half an hour when he noticed his father's head begin to drift across the back of the seat. He started the motor and headed back to town. His father went downhill quickly after that, and he died a few weeks later. Folks found it strange that his mother didn't seem to grieve much after the funeral, but that was just the way she was. It was over—time to get on with things.

He wasn't looking forward to his own appointment with the doctor this morning, either. His wife had been after him for months, and he'd finally relented. She'd made the appointment, and he had to admit he felt somewhat relieved knowing he'd soon find out—one way or another—so that he, too, could get on with things.

He decided to skip breakfast. He knew he wouldn't be able to relax enough to sit down and eat so he figured there was no point—and, anyway, his stomach was still bothering him. He made himself a mug of instant coffee instead to take outside with him when he went to turn on the garden sprinkler. He would eat later with his wife after he'd seen the doctor. She'd wanted to go with him, but he hadn't been comfortable with that. If the news was bad, he'd need some time to digest it.

After he got the sprinkler going, he went over to the machine shed and backed out the old Massey Harris tractor and wagon load of hay and drove it behind he barn to feed the cattle. When he was growing up, they'd had dairy cattle, pigs, chickens—a little bit of everything. They'd even had work horses—huge Clydesdales he used to ride bareback before the tractor came. Then his father sold the horses to the glue factory—no point feeding an animal which wasn't doing any work. It was the same with the barn cats. A few were needed to control rats and mice, and the rest (usually kittens) were put in burlap bags weighted down with rocks and taken down to the creek. His father did it at first, but by the time he was twelve it had become his job. It had been a hard farm to work with thin soil. Now he had a job at the mill and just ran these few head of beef, and the only cats were stray toms.

He went back to the house and, after turning off the sprinkler, began watering the red geraniums banked around the house. It used to be said that, if the barn was well maintained and the house unpainted with no time wasted on flowers, the man was in charge. If there were flowers, either the woman was boss or they were rich. Well—his barn was a mess, and his wife had insisted the house be painted before she'd move in.

After he showered and changed his clothes, he was anxious to leave, even though it wasn't yet nine o'clock and his appointment was at ten. Town was less than fifteen minutes away, but he decided to go ahead anyway. He could always grab a coffee at the restaurant across from the doctor's office.

As he crossed the yard, he wondered if he should take the gun out of the truck. It made his wife nervous, she said, sitting with a loaded gun behind her head. Her cousin had shot himself in the foot one Sunday afternoon as he sat cleaning his gun on the front porch. An uncle of hers had shot himself—on purpose, too—so he really couldn't blame her. He thought that maybe he should take it out then remembered he'd just changed, and taking the gun down to the dusty old barn where she insisted he keep it would make him dirty.

Suddenly, the stillness of the morning was broken by the sound of a vehicle coming down the gravel road, and he turned to see twin plumes of dust heading down the concession road towards his lane, then past. He stared at the wisps of dust rising like thin brown clouds. Then he got into the truck and headed out.

When he reached the highway he signalled right towards town but kept his foot on the brakes. When someone behind him honked, he signalled left and pulled out onto the highway. Two hundred metres further along, he turned right onto a dirt road which ran alongside a gravel pit. It was the same place he'd taken his father. He drove about a quarter mile to where the road made a ninety degree turn then backed onto an old logging track. He turned off the motor and rolled down his window. In the distance, he could hear a flock of crows fighting over something.

Later that day, a young girl on horseback cantered down a country road towards a grove of maples. As the horse moved out of the sunlight and into the wooded area, she could make out a pickup truck parked near the road with the driver's side door open. As she drew closer, she saw what seemed to be a pair of feet on the ground beneath the open door.

Widow

She had driven up to his home. Half an hour both ways. I won't miss this trek. She felt lighthearted. This is how it should have been, how it should always feel. Light. I feel light.

She had driven up to his home to give him a butterfly kiss. What's this? she will ask, eyelashes fluttering on his thin cheek. What's this? Later that year a blue butterfly—I'm telling you, as big as my hand— flies into her hair. Instinctually she will brush at it, get away. It's him, she will think, watching it from above as it pumps its good wing. Tears welling in her eyes as she tells the story. It was beautiful.

She had driven up to his home only to find him slumped on his front steps. And everything fell away everywhere at once. Like turning on a light and discovering that you are in a cavernous room. Yes, like that, but the opposite. And you are small. So small. Familiar steering wheel, grooves for your fingers, how convenient. Growing flowers, damp soil. That was sweet of him to keep the flowerbeds watered. She gets out and starts walking. Now she is running. He had said, sighing inaudibly, looking tired, I don't want to disappoint you. One stroke already, perceptible to the eye that knew, had left him soft. Blinking like a twitch, they had looked at each other.

Now standing with his family, hers. A minister is talking about something. Pray for me Father, her hand tugging his sleeve. Pray that I will have the strength to get through this. Knees unaccustomed to kneeling near to buckling under the impulse to make a scene. Look at this. Small her holding a small yellow chick in her cupped hands, raising it like a chalice. *Far, jeg tænke* ... It's not ... Eyes wide staring blindly. Did I do this? An odd inside-out sensation. Like she was everywhere but inside herself. Like everything was nothing except for a vague awareness that this was the case. A yellow chick. Hers to look after. To love. To hold. Not too hard, Meta. Shouldn't he be in robes or something? Metallic calm catching her off guard. Strange, everyone is talking again. She lets go of the sleeve. Plaid.

I am not some woman from the desert wailing over her terrorist husband's body, she thinks to herself at the funeral. This helps as well. People's eyes fly open and dart at each other in panic when she starts to cry and can't stop. Fine. She decides not to accept the drinks pushed on her by the well-meaning. Trying to swallow has become like trying to inhale a strong wind. She imagines herself standing on sand, the dry wind whipping her clothes, lifting then flattening her permed hair. She feels so dry her face aches. This will work, she thinks, but when she looks up at the picture of him in his black suit and red bowtie, their Caribbean wedding with only some locals who were in the business, waves and waves of grief crash over her again. Tears well up and spring smoothly down her cheek in tidy contempt for her heroics, for the ocean that has swirled up around her. She lets out a weak sliding cry in spite of herself. A man she doesn't recognize puts an arm around her. Get off, she thinks but instead sinks into his chest and remains there, rocking slightly.

You don't get long on this Earth, and you don't get much, and what you do get you don't get for long. She has begun to think in looping platitudes. They have lost what little comfort they had brought, but she can't stop. Like how she can't stop moving. Not even a week after the funeral, and she has already been to the dentist, got her early retirement papers in order, and managed to get her house back from the new owner. Such a nice man, but I think he has skin cancer because he's always had a little bandage on his forehead. You never know when it's your turn. But you keep going. She stands up suddenly and walks to her car. A gift. She finds herself in a store buying a cement lawn ornament of a little boy with wings. She tells the girl at the cash, barely seventeen and easily flustered, that her husband just died and she's going to put this by the birdbath. The girl says *oh* and then rings it in quickly. It's expensive, she thinks, but you get what you pay for.

Someone has sent her white flowers. Her neighbour, the nosy one always peering over the fence, has taken them off her doorstep. Keep the vase. She brings them inside and puts them beside the remaining arrangements. The white makes her feel still. She looks at the other flowers. Their colour schemes clash and sound like a hundred people talking all at once in different accents. Get out. She picks up a vase and throws it across the room. It doesn't break but bounces off the couch, spilling water, orange petals, and green stems onto the carpet. And that seemed to make me just lose it, she will say later with a thin half-smile and a shake of her head. Some big affront. She races over to the vase and throws it onto the tiles. It shatters. With a glissando of vowels she pushes four more off a table. Another vase refuses to break. She takes it to the front door and throws it onto the driveway, where it bursts with a satisfying pop, fragments skidding over the sidewalk and onto the road. She has cut her hand and, notices later, her foot. Quite badly. I'm so clumsy, she tells the doctor, sounding like she's protecting someone. He looks at her closely, his white jacket making him fade into the white walls. She enjoys his concern but says, I'm a widow.

Skin

In March 1978 the weekly magazines in Paris were full of features remembering the political events of the spring of 1968. One evening Claire McGibbon sat in the kitchen of an apartment in a high rise on the Boulevard Pasteur, reading the *Nouvel Observateur* and eating butter cookies. The butter cookies were a problem. She had not bought them herself but was taking them from the tin where M. Gibranski had put them. He ate one or two in the afternoons with a cup of Assam tea during a break between patients. The cookies, the tin, the apartment itself belonged to M. Gibranski. Claire had a room of her own and use of the bathroom and the kitchen in exchange for looking after his children in the afternoons. What should have been the sitting room was M. Gibranski's office; the little room that she had to pass through to leave or enter the apartment was the waiting room, windowless, with a fan of magazines on a table and a series of African masks on the wall.

M. Gibranski was a Lacanian analyst. One of the Dutch au pairs at the Sorbonne told Claire that this meant that he only saw his patients for fifteen minutes and would say nothing during that time. What kind of unhappiness would bring a person to submit to that? M. Gibranski was charming and severe in his manner, asking after her French course, her family, her impressions of Paris—and reminding her of the rules. She was to be absent from the apartment every weekday afternoon between 12:00 and 17:00, so that he might see patients. She was to leave nothing in the waiting room, not a pair of shoes, not a book. If the telephone should ring, she was to answer it and take careful notes without revealing her identity to the caller. Should she see M. Gibranski in the hallway or the elevator with someone else, she was not to acknowledge him.

He did not live in the apartment. He lived on the floor below with his wife and the two children. The oldest, Olivier, was his son from a previous marriage, and the baby, Séraphim, belonged to them both. His wife, talking on the phone with friends, would say, "It's very difficult now with two children..." while Claire sat on the floor with the baby in her lap, playing chess with Olivier.

She had some time alone with Séraphim every day before she had to fetch Olivier from school. When she had first laid eyes on the baby she had thought him a homely infant, pasty, disorganized looking. But over the winter she had fallen in love with him and now viewed his fattening legs and his deep eyes with pleasure. She leaned over him in his pram, holding his gaze and saying "You little devil" to make him laugh. One day the femme de ménage had asked him, "Where's your maman?" and he had looked at Claire, not at his mother. Claire described incidents like this in letters to her boyfriend in Montreal. She also described both apartments, M. and Mme. Gibranski and the children, and the Dutch and English au pairs at the university. The boyfriend wrote back to tell her what he was reading and what he thought about what he was reading, ending always with a paragraph about his desire for her. These final paragraphs were generally unsatisfactory to Claire, blunt and formulaic. When she read them she could not remember what it was like to touch her boyfriend.

She ate all of the butter cookies. She would now have to travel to Poilane's in the morning, before her classes, to buy more cookies to replace these. She licked a finger and pressed it into the crumbs at the rim of the tin, trying to remember exactly how many cookies had been there when she started. Then she left the kitchen and walked deliberately into the office, shutting the door behind her before she turned on a lamp. Usually the extent of her evening transgression was to lie where the patients lay—on the chaise longue in the office—and study the art on the walls: more African masks, carpets with holes in them, and one painting of a volcano. But this evening she sat in the chair at the desk and noticed a sheet of paper in the type-writer. The roller clicked as she wound it forward, to read: *Hier soir j'ai dit à mon amante, ma peau t'aime.*

My skin loves you. In grade seven, no lovers in sight, Claire had once watched an older girl waiting for the school bus with her boyfriend on a grass verge. The girl had leaned towards him and taken the point of his shirt collar between her teeth. This was like that. She rolled the line back into place and went to lie down on the pony skin of the chaise longue.

The next afternoon, alone with Séraphim in the family apartment, Claire lay suspended in a hammock slung between two metal supports on the terrace. Séraphim was sitting on her lap, wearing pyjamas and a cardigan. A Bob Dylan record played on the stereo, the speakers turned to face the terrace. Claire unzipped her jacket, pulled up her Shetland sweater, and unbuttoned her shirt. She adjusted Séraphim so that his warmth covered the skin of her belly. It was hard to know how long he might be happy like that, but the music would help to prolong his patience. He was still smiling and prodding her when M. Gibranski came into the apartment and out onto the terrace, frowning, saying that he must talk to her.

He began by saying that he believed he had been quite clear about the rules. Claire shifted Séraphim on her lap and tried to sit up in the hammock. The movement twisted her corduroy skirt higher on her legs and exposed the chapped flesh of her knees. The skin of her face and neck flushed. "You left this in the waiting room," he said, holding out a blue airmail envelope addressed to her, a letter from the boyfriend. "The patients will have read this, they will have drawn conclusions. Are you unaware of the damage this can do?" No, not unaware she said, although she did not understand how reading the address on an envelope might damage anyone. He was twisting his hair in one hand. Really sorry. She must have put it down while putting on her shoes, and then forgotten it. "You cannot forget. This is very serious," he said. He bent down and lifted Séraphim off her lap and, holding him with one arm, pinched the fat of his cheek while still concentrating his attention on Claire. "Nothing in the waiting room," he said, now circling Séraphim's head with his hand. "But don't get up; there is no need," and as she began to swing her legs over the edge of the hammock he deposited the baby back on her lap. "All is well here?" he asked then, moving his eyes away from the gap in her shirt, and searching for a way to end the conversation. "All is well," said Claire, pulling down her sweater, shielded by Séraphim.

Barry, It's Alright

Well, Barry, the reason I come is that I wanna get things straight as a doornail. Sure, I'll have another beer. Surly lookin' cur of a waiter, ain't he?

Well there I was, putting up my feet after I come in off the back forty, sitting with a beer as pretty as a groundhog in a winter burrow, thinkin' maybe I'll catch the last period of the hockey game, when what do you think the wind blew in? The front doorbell began to ring its head off, ringing and dinging and irritating as hell. I've got half a mind to shoot the damn thing. It's the only thing around the place that really is useless. And you know me. I have a use for everything. I was telling the guy at the slaughterhouse the other day that, when I butcher hogs, I use every part of the carcass except the asshole, which I send down the road as a salesman. Careful, Barry, you're spillin' beer on your Hudson's Bay suit. Figured that'd cheer you up.

"Hey, boy, my gullet's dry!" What's that, Barry? I'm supposed to say "gar-sun"? You say it. I'll drink it.

So anyways, there I was, thinkin' about my farrowing sow and about how I'm not gonna be able to cheat too much on my taxes this year what with the new government forms and the fact that a guy really can't claim too many deductions with a scraggy lot of bush hogs that ain't never, and we're talking Judgement Day here, gonna bring more than a plugged nickel at the next auction in town. I think I'll go down to the pulp mill and start buying Number 2 chipboard to feed 'em, for all the meat they're puttin' on their bones.

No, next round's on me. C'mon, one more ain't gonna hurt ya. You're far from being a basket case, like the wife's brother. "Hold yer horses," I says to that doorbell, "while I get my slippers."

"Jesus Tapdancin' Christ," I says to Maggie, "who could that be at this time of night? It's colder than an accountant's heart out there, and it can't be my brother-in-law. He's been on a drunk down at the Legion Hall for the past month."

I put out my pipe on the back of my hand, and I headed to the door. Damn thing's sticking again. I'll have to get the plane out of the milkshed and scrape a quarter-inch off the bottom. When I opened that door, Barry, I damn near started fartin' backwards, if you catch my drift. There, standing on the snowbank, was *The Wife*. Last I heard, she was at your place. I damn near fell on my Royal Canadian ass. Well, let me tell you, I started to hummin' and hawin' to beat the band. I made out like I didn't know her from a bale of hay, pretending to be snowblind.

"Honey," she says, "it's me, Leslie." Something wrong with the beer, Barry? You're lookin' a mite shaky.

There she was, the wind driftin' around her Skidoo boots. "Lester?" I says, stallin' for time. "The only Lester I know is the former prime minister, Lester B. Pearson, but you can't be him, him bein' dead and all."

"No, Leslie," she says. "Heavens to Betsy, let me in."

"Wipe yer feet," I says, trying to remain calm and collected, even though I sure as hell wasn't calm and the only thing I knew I'd collect would be a hard smack on the kisser. The wife ain't blind, and, even if she was, she could still see clear through me like river ice in April, so I knew I'd have to explain *The Other Woman*. Hold on, Barry, don't interrupt. Put yer jaw back into idle.

"Maggie," I says, "this here's the wife."

"Pleased to meet you," says Maggie.

"Well now," says the wife, all hoity toity, "aren't you full of piss and vinegar? What a charming pair, Ross and Aphromighty. I come back to see if maybe we can work things out, but I think I'll just collect my things. I go off *en ville*"—that's the wife's way of sayin' she's high tailin' it into town, she's been to school and all; the way she says it, it kinda rhymes with windasill—"I go off *en ville* and leave you to keep the home fires burning, but *Monsooer* here lights up a regular little forest fire."

"Now Leslie," I says, "fair's fair. I put up with your brother's drinking, and I knew you was feelin' frustrated out here in the weeds what with your education and all, so I let you go off and visit my brother Barry and hobnob all over hell's half acre, but, you gotta admit, six months is a long vacation. A man's got to go on living, and when there's nobody next to ya under them Fortrel sheets, well ... I took up with Maggie here 'cause I got to thinkin' you'd never come back."

"I had to find myself," she says, "and that takes time. I love you and I respect you—until now that is, talk about a cheap hussy—but I am my own woman with my own life to live."

"That's just jim dandy," I says, "but I got alfalfa and rye and a pig barn to look after, and I can't afford to go galavantin' around findin' myself. Maybe I don't want to, or maybe I was never lost. This farm's important to me and to Maggie, too. She's worth two field hands and a backhoe, the way she helps out. We get along real well, and she don't have no drunken brother. She's just my cup of tea, if ya catch my meanin'."

"Oh, I do," she says, "and I'm suing for divorce. I come out here to pick up the pieces, but I can see that the vase is beyond repair. It's obvious you don't want me. Well, pas de problemy in that department! You're not the only man around, you know. By the way, I had an affair with your brother Barry. *Among others!*" she yells as she takes off, but the damn door stuck again and I had to yard it open. She was so hot she yanked off my John Deere cap and stomped on it for good measure.

So that's it. Now, Barry, don't apologize. It'll make your beer taste sour. Looks like we're loaded for bear now, don't it? I just want you to know there ain't no hard feelings on my part. What's done is done. I don't suppose you did nothin' but what any man in your position woulda done. Yes, I will have another beer. "Gar-sun, another round, and make it snappy!"

I woulda come to see you sooner, but the road hasn't been ploughed—guess we'll have to wait till the next election. I had to put chains on the tractor just to make it to the main highway. Barry, it's alright, *I assure you*, as the wife would say. What we had is gone, but there's no use cryin' over spilt milk. I hope the wife is happy. Drink up.

How to Be

I was called home early from camp the summer of '48. My grandfather was waiting for me at the train station. He was more solemn than usual, and, as we walked along the overhead bridge of the train tracks, my mind darted through other summers, when, as a small child, we took this route to pick up the evening paper, when this same walk could also mean a movie or an ice-cream cone, and I went, hoping.

But not tonight. Tonight, Grandad was walking much more briskly, and, when he took my hand, something he rarely ever did, I could feel the solemnity, the importance of this evening, and I tried to react as he would want me to. It bothered me that I spent so much time acting as I was expected to act. It hadn't been so bad when I was little, but now I was fifteen!

Grandad's voice was gruff, which by itself didn't alarm me, but his total manner seemed so unlike him.

"Try to be of some comfort to your mother," I heard him say, and I thought to myself, How do most people show comfort? I guessed it meant touching? To be sort of soothing? But I supposed that, to my mother, it meant no arguing, to answer her letters promptly, and to "be a good girl." Long ago, I had learned that any outward expression of affection between my mother and me seemed somehow uncomfortable. So how could I show comfort with both of us feeling uncomfortable?

Still, I nodded, to show him that I heard, and, as we passed the Fraleigh house on the corner and turned towards my grandparents' home, I studied my grandfather's new gait, his hat at a jauntier angle than I'd remembered. His bearing belied his eighty-two years, and suddenly I wondered if he, too, was considering the unfairness of it all—that he should be so fit, so vital, when at that moment my father, his son-in-law, was in an oxygen tent, somewhere in Detroit.

My grandfather never really approved of my father, I could tell. For years, I'd believed they were both strong men and that was why they never really got along. I'd been told the story many times, of how my mother, at twenty-three, couldn't decide whether she should marry my father or Reddrick, a boy she'd gone all through school with and the son of my grandparents' best friends. It was while she was studying in Toronto that she'd planned to elope with Reddrick, only to be brought home by a fake telegram stating: MOTHER ILL. COME HOME AT ONCE. Dutifully, she did, only to find it wasn't true. Then later, when she went to her aunt's in Chicago, to decide, finally, who her husband would be, with the understanding that neither of her "beaux" would try to contact her, somehow my father was able to pry the phone number from my grandfather, and it was that magic phone call that determined her choice. Every time I heard that story, I marveled that anyone could pry anything out of my grandfather, unless, of course, he wanted it that way. My mother believed it was Daddy's charm that made Grandad give in, and maybe she was right. Still, none of this jibed with Grandad's current disapproval, and I often wished they liked each other, partly because I was afraid Grandad's disapproval extended to me, too, and partly because I loved them both.

The memory of that story made me take another look at Grandad, still walking at the same fast clip, only this time, I was thinking about his fake telegram and the phone number he'd "reluctantly" produced for my father, so many years ago. Wow, I thought, what if what I'm seeing is someone who knows he shouldn't have done that, that if it hadn't been for him...

"I really don't think there's anything to laugh about, young lady!"

He let go of my hand and began searching for his house key. In my shame, I concentrated on his gently pudgy fingers putting the key all the way in, then pulling it out slightly, then turning it and the doorknob at the same time. Feeling the sudden gush of cold air in the darkness of the hallway gave me a moment to realign my features, a second chance, and I was grateful that we couldn't see each other.

I followed the smell of Aqua Velva through the hall and into the dining room. Grandad turned the lights on and took off his hat, all in one gesture, then he headed towards the kitchen. Wearily, he sat down near the phone.

"I'm expecting a telephone call from your mother. She said she'd phone from the hospital." He took out his pocket watch to check it against the clock in the dining room. "Should be any minute now, child, and then we'll know what the word is."

I recognized his reference to me as "child." I felt better. I went into the adjoining den and took in a deep breath of Lilies of the Valley and National Geographic. It had been years since I'd stayed with my grandparents. I found myself in front of the mirror over the couch. I was surprised that so much of me was reflected in it. I could remember when I had to kneel on the couch to even see my forehead. Again, I knelt, as I began my ruthless examination: my hair, still in braids, but at least they were pinned up now; my forehead was too wide, and it bulged. I wished I could pluck my eyebrows. Still, I had no real pimples and at a certain angle, if the light was right, and it was, I had cheekbones. That's good, I told myself. I compared my face with the pictures on either side of the mirror. One of my mother, the other of her younger sister. I looked a bit like my aunt, but I would rather have looked like my mother. I loosened one of my braids and tried to push it into a wave, like hers. It dipped limply onto my forehead. It didn't help. Somehow, she had an ethereal quality, like the Lady of Shalott or Myrna Loy, and that was something I knew I'd never have. I reconsidered my Aunt Kay, looking so sturdy, so capable in her nurse's cap. I wondered if a cap like that might help me. I looked again at my mother's picture. This time I noticed her hands, her long curved fingernails. The photographer's lights mistily highlighted the shine of her nail polish. I'd never really thought of her hands this way before. It was as if the photographer knew her secret: that she'd never had any serious intention of becoming a pianist. This thought was not entirely unfounded, I'd often heard her say she'd never been consulted. Then I thought of Grandad and the conservatory, and all that money, and I wondered if he, too, had ever noticed those beautiful hands, those long, defiant fingernails.

My posing ended abruptly when the phone rang. Quietly, I edged my way towards it. Grandad still treated a long-distance call as an event to be respected with absolute silence. At first, I thought I'd startled him, or was it the news he was reacting to? I carefully watched his face, looking for new furrows, wondering if that habit of slowly pressing his moustache with his thumb meant anything in particular. His voice was muffled, still gruff, becoming almost inaudible. I think he said she should stay there as long as she thought it was necessary, that she wasn't to worry about a thing, that they'd look after me. As he said that, he was looking right at me and I heard him say, "She's here now. Would you like to talk with her?"

He beckoned sharply (he hadn't forgotten it was long distance). I was about to take the receiver, but first he warned me not to say anything to upset her. I nodded.

"Hello? Mummy? How's Daddy?" The voice, coming from so far away, didn't sound at all like my mother's. She sounded so small. But I was careful not to mention this.

"I guess Grandad has already told you that your Dad has had a coronary ... a heart attack?"

"Well, I knew he was in an oxygen tent."

"Probably he didn't want to worry you."

"Well, is he okay now?"

"The doctors still have him in intensive care, so naturally he's on the critical list, so at this point we just won't know for a while what's what."

"You mean he could *die*?"

Grandad promptly jerked the phone away from me. I knew

he was saying goodbye for me. I also knew I shouldn't have asked that last question. I hadn't meant to.

The room was quiet again. Grandad didn't (or wouldn't?) look at me. He put the receiver back on the hook and went to the pantry. From there, I was offered a glass of milk.

"No, thank you. I think I'll just go up now. Does it matter which bedroom I use?"

"Take whichever one you'd like."

"Then I'll take the front bedroom," I said, remembering the eiderdown that went with that room.

I sidled towards him and kissed him on the cheek. Again, more Aqua Velva, this time, with the prickle of his evening whiskers, strangely softer than usual, and then I remembered my half-braided, half-loose hair. I must have looked pretty funny, but perhaps he hadn't noticed.

"Goodnight, m'dear, sleep tight. And about your dad..." His voice trailed off. I paused to wait while he finished.

"Yes?" I said, carefully.

"It's a damned shame," he answered.

I found my way up the winding stairs. I thought about that room with the eiderdown, where I used to have so many naps, when lots of times I didn't sleep, believing I could read those blurs of words. I thought about another word for eiderdown: comforter. How could I be that for her? I could hear my shoes, slow to leave each step. The varnish always did that in the summertime.

Landings

Every day but Sunday Anna Cavallo, who lives in a small one-bedroom apartment in the city's east end, takes the metro home from work, walks two blocks from the station, and climbs three flights of stairs. This isn't easy, for her legs are failing and tend to go weak and trembly when she climbs stairs. It isn't too bad when her arms are empty, but today she is carrying two bags of groceries.

She pauses halfway up the first flight. She could rest here, but this stairwell is dingier than the others. The walls are grimy yellow and chipped in pieces, exposing dirty plaster. The only smooth space bears a crudely drawn heart with an arrow piercing it, above crooked letters saying *Olivia Loves Manuel*. Anna doesn't know what she thinks of this. It's touching, but she doesn't approve of people writing on walls.

Who could have drawn it puzzles her. There are no Olivias or Manuels in this building, or anyone of an age to scribble on walls. Besides herself, there are only Mr. Khan, who walks with a cane, and the Pulaski sisters, who are too old to have children. The scribblers must have sneaked in from the street. She hopes they came only to kiss and cuddle, and only once—it was scary that it might be so easy to get in. She climbs to the second floor, where she sets her groceries on the top step and sits down beside them.

She has worked hard today, at Mrs. Adams's on Montclair in the morning and Mrs. Leicester's in the afternoon. Both were sticklers for little things, polishing in particular. Mrs. Adams collected brass ornaments, and Mrs. Leicester owls and elephants. Each one had to be individually dusted, as did the slats of Mrs. Adams's blinds.

Her hands hurt. She holds them up for inspection. The fingers don't extend straight out any more; the knuckles are permanently bent and remarkably wrinkled. She tries to flex them, to remind them how they used to be. Her back also aches. She eases it against the wall opposite the Pulaski's door. She hopes they won't be shocked if they look through the peep hole and see her. She hopes they haven't heard her footsteps stop and think someone's come to do them harm.

Anna doesn't know the Pulaskis, not even whether they speak English. If she sees them in the lobby they smile and bob their heads, but neither has ever said hello. She doesn't know their first names, only the letters "G" and "I" on their mailbox; which is which, or what the letters stand for, she has no idea.

The landing is permeated today with the odour of cooked cabbage, which the sisters seem to eat a lot of. Anna associates the smell with humiliation; it's what they used to serve in the orphanage. The smell somehow embarrasses her. She wants to escape it, but she's too tired to get up. She decides instead to try to play her game.

She settles against the wall and closes her eyes, summoning the image of the garden where she meets the old woman. She doesn't have a name, she is simply "the old woman," a figure Anna invented one day when she was scrubbing someone's floor. She resembles no-one Anna knows, certainly not her mother, who died when Anna was seven. The woman in the garden is thin, with pale, crinkled skin and smooth white hair. She moves about the grounds with deliberation, gliding from roses to dahlias to columbine, as if performing a graceful, slow-motion dance. Occasionally she stops and buries her face in one of the flowers. This is Anna's favourite part, for through the old woman's eyes she can peer deep inside the flower's scarlet throat and see the golden stamens swaying expectantly, their tips quivering with pollen. She breathes deeply of it, letting the cool petals caress her cheek. But the cabbage odour interferes. She sighs, gathers her packages, and pushes herself to her feet.

Sixteen steps, then Mr. Khan's landing. Here she rests again. She retrieves an apple from her bag and holds it against her cheek, using its cool, smooth feel to return to the game.

Sometimes it doesn't work; the old woman is not present, or is difficult to locate. This time Anna finds her easily. She is sitting on a white wrought-iron chair, wearing a lavender dress with lace around the wrists and neck. In her hand is a Chinese fan with delicate birds painted on it.

The old woman can't see Anna, of course; she has never so much as glanced in Anna's direction. Instead she gazes across the garden to a tree beyond the hedge. Anna follows her gaze to a small slender birch tree. It is lovely but, to Anna's eyes, perfectly ordinary. She wonders if the woman can see something in it she can't. Anna stares at it, hard, but then a fly buzzes around her head. She opens her eyes and flaps at it angrily. The woman was directing her to the tree for some reason, and now she may never find out what it was. She feels robbed.

Dear God, she thinks suddenly, where is her purse? She glances around wildly but doesn't see it. Has she left it on a lower landing? Panic fills her. She searches the grocery bags, removing soup cans, grapefruit, boxes of crackers ... but of course it isn't there. She tries to remember what she was carrying when she left the market, but all her arms recall are the groceries.

She pounds down the stairs, but it isn't on any of the landings, nor is it in the lobby. She runs into the street, her heart hammering. It's been stolen, she is convinced, and with it a full day's wages.

As she crosses the street she feels a spasm of pain, like a spurt of liquid fire racing up her chest and down her arm. She gasps. The next instant she is flat on the pavement, unable to move. She is aware of shapes moving around her, twittering, but their language is as mysterious as birdsong. She can't see well, but oddly she isn't worried. She tries to tell the shapes not to make a fuss, but the words won't form.

She closes her eyes, and the garden returns. The old woman is still sitting there, her hands folded in her lap. For the first time she turns and looks directly at Anna before letting her eyes rest on the tree beyond the hedge.

Anna sees it shining in the sun. It must have just rained; the vivid green leaves, dripping with water, are glowing as if lit from within. Something seems to be swaying in its branches, but she can't make it out; it is the same bright green, sparkling with light. Ah, she thinks in wonder, it's the snake, but the tree and the snake aren't separate: they are a single whole.

She turns to the old woman to share this revelation, but the garden has faded. Only the tree still glows, as if gathering into itself what is left of the light. She gazes at it, rapt, until it, too, fades.

2004-2005

What about Us?

When Lou and Bonnie disappeared into the quaking aspens we were at a birthday bonfire at the beach. As is the custom, the birthday boy was tossed into the water, and then someone said, "Hey, where did Lou disappear to?"

"We saw him talking to Bonnie."

"Maybe they went to get more wood."

"Maybe."

We figured they had slipped into the darkness to smoke a joint away from the kids. A dark night it was, too. Since there was no moon, the stars dangled like crystals.

Those who found Lou and Bonnie should have read the signs. Like there was no hint of pot, and back in the firelight their faces looked pretty red.

A few days later we began to worry. It was during the end of summer Band Jam. When Lou wasn't playing mandolin, he was sitting at Bonnie's table. When Lou was playing mandolin he stared at Bonnie, who smiled the whole damned time.

Someone shouted, "When is Karen coming back?"

"Not soon enough."

Lou's wife, Karen, was off training in Hotel Management. Bonnie's Ben had just left for South Carolina with his rig loaded with blueberries.

We took it upon ourselves to help our friends. We would handle it very delicately. Those of us closest to Karen and Lou (four kids, survivors of twenty years together) would tackle Lou. Those of us who had always known Bonnie and Ben (married forever, two teenage boys) would reason with Bonnie.

"What the hell do you think you're doing?"

"We're just good friends."

"We're all good friends. How much better friends do you need to be?"

We found ourselves in a very awkward position. Like the time Karen phoned looking for Lou.

"Lou? He was just here."

"Oh good. I couldn't reach him at home, and the kids had no clue."

We all felt guilty but decided it was right not to raise suspicions over what might just be a crush. Who among us hadn't had those? Besides, Lou really had been here. True, that was over three hours ago, but we weren't the police. We wished Ben and Karen would hurry up and come home.

There was another complication. What was supposed to be only a few of us who knew about the situation had grown. Some of us were losing sleep with worry and had felt a need to confide in others. Now there were phone calls happening all over town.

"What's the latest on, you know?"

"I saw them at the video store. Acting like they'd just bumped into each other."

Or:

"I just heard something weird about Bonnie and Lou. Is it true?"

"Uh, well, I guess I can tell you. You won't say anything."

"Of course not. You know that."

Any hopes that nothing truly serious was going on were dashed when we caught Lou and Bonnie out behind the tavern being serious indeed. Some of us took Lou by the arm and some of us Bonnie, and we hauled them into the light of the parking lot.

"Is this a midlife crisis? Because you're acting like kids."

"And speaking of kids, have you even thought about yours?"

"Do you know how horrible this is for us?"

It was quite simple, they said. They were soulmates. Yes, of course they loved Karen and Ben, too, but they couldn't stop this any more than one can stop the tide. Try harder, we advised them.

When Karen came back, right away she knew something was wrong. Lou seemed so distant. We admitted he had seemed pretty stressed. Anything interesting happen while she was away? Not really. Pretty boring, really. We looked at each other. Who would she kill first? Him? Her? Or us?

Then things seemed to settle down. Bonnie left town to visit her mom, and Karen said she and Lou were enjoying each other's company for the first time in months.

Summer was over. One of us went back to the city where she lives when she isn't here. She phoned at least once a week just to see how everyone was. All we had to report was that there was a concern over a Visa bill from a motel in the next town where Lou and Bonnie had been spotted last month. We were debating whether or not to stake out her mailbox before she got to it. Why? Because we were hoping the affair was over. We thought the big lesson to learn here was that a marriage is fragile and sometimes needs a little help from friends. Right?

Wrong. Karen dropped in one night. Had we seen Lou? He hadn't come home for supper. Had she tried him at work? He's a mail carrier, she reminded us. We felt like idiots. Of course, Bonnie had returned yesterday.

"Someone has to tell her," said our friend in the city.

"Easy for you to say. But how do you tell someone that her husband is having an affair and that her friends have known for weeks?"

"Tricky," she agreed. "By the way, I knew nothing about it, right?"

As it turned out, Lou told Karen. Some of it, at least. He took her for Chinese food and said he wanted out. When she showed up in tears, we asked if he had told her why. She nodded. Apparently he'd wanted out for a very long time, but hadn't had the nerve to say.

Someone handed Karen a beer.

"That's it? You didn't wonder why he has the nerve now?"

"You mean another woman? That was my first question, but he said no."

Now we had to tell her. So we did. No-one mentioned the Visa bill, but we confessed to knowing about this mess all along. We made it clear that we were on Karen's side. And poor Ben's, too.

Ben had barely jumped down from his truck when Bonnie told him about her and Lou. We held our breaths, wondering what Ben might do. But all he did was march over to Karen's house with a bottle of Kahlua, and they stayed under a blanket until dawn.

"You're joking!" screamed our friend when she phoned from the city. "Karen and Ben? This is too much! What about Lou and Bonnie?"

"They'll find out soon enough."

We felt that everyone should know. It seemed only fair to their kids. Hell, even our own kids were traumatized by the news.

Yes, it has been quite confusing for everyone, seeing Lou's car in Bonnie's driveway and Ben's truck parked in front of Karen's house. They've even traded around some of the kids. The worst is that they all seem to tingle with an energy none of us have felt in years. We imagine they have their moments of grief or guilt, but they insist this is the best thing to have ever happened. This whole thing makes our own marriages seem like an awful lot of work.

J.D. McDonald

Dance of the Moondogs

Jesus I was strong in them days, with muscles all hard and new jumping right out of my shoulders and legs long enough to run me right out of sight. School was hell though, so I quit as soon as I could, which wasn't soon enough for me 'cause I'd sat there doing nothing for so goddamn long anyway. Most of us had. And the teachers were always the same, just staring into the faces of forty Indian Kids and looking as uncomfortable as hell.

The day me and a bunch of others decided to quit was after we'd lit a little fire in the back seat of this teacher's car, whose name I don't remember, and he'd come running into the classroom for some water shouting and cursing and calling us friggin' savages and the like. We just laughed out loud 'cause he looked all pinched and red-faced with this big tie knotted up around his throat, as if to choke the life right out of him. So a bunch of us just figured that we'd had enough and that there was no point in hanging around there anymore.

Sure there was some government guy who came around to see my mother to tell her that me and my brother had to be in school because that was the law and so that we could get good paying jobs and all that. But none of us Indians believed that bullshit since we'd never seen any member of our band make any money by his education. The only one we'd ever heard of who got rich was an Indian who went to California to be in the pictures and after that he never came back even to say hello to his old friends and brothers. We'd see him when we went to the movies on Saturday afternoon at the Beaver down in town. Most of the time he got killed along with a lot of other guys who didn't look very Indian to me. They were just kind of painted the right colour.

It was April, and the sun was dandelion yellow and as warm as a chimney brick when you stood out in it. There was still even snow hiding in the bush under the black skirts of big cedars and pines. We all thought it was a great time to be free from peering into the white pages of books to find out what happened to white people instead of having it happen to us. So we spent a couple of weeks camping in the bush just watching the rest of winter melt, feeling the world turn all crazy green right under our feet. At night I watched the spring stars and they looked like a bunch of frozen beads of water on a wool blanket. I can remember just lying in my bedroll waiting for one of those stars to break loose and fall deep into the forest, because my father told me that, if an Indian kid could find the place the star fell, he'd see a huge white moose with blue eyes born right out of that fallen star.

If a star fell out of the sky during the time we were in the bush I guess I missed it. But I do remember getting excited when I woke up sudden one night, my head leaping with bad dreams and saw all the stars wobbling in the sky as if every one of them was going to shower down on my head. Jumping Jesus I had the shit scared out of me! I could imagine thousands of white moose getting born all around and me so amazed that I wouldn't know what to do because that was the part of the story that my father always forgot. The sky tried to shake loose all those stars but they hung on and not even one fell to the ground in my dark forest. Soon the night stopped trembling and I was one relieved Indian kid.

After that we left the bush and went back to the Reserve to try to figure out what to do. Johnnie Black was the first to make up his mind and he decided he'd go to Toronto and get a job on construction and get $1.20 an hour. Most of us figured that kind of money was dreaming because it added up to near $90 a week for an Indian kid of seventeen or eighteen. But he told us he had heard all about jobs like that in town from some old man who read the newspapers almost every day. He wore spectacles with only one piece of glass and said that because the war was over there was a need to build some place to put everybody coming back from the fighting. That didn't make no sense to me, because I heard from one of those teachers that there was a lot of people killed in the war so it seemed to me that fewer soldiers would be coming back than went.

Johnnie didn't understand what I was talking about though and said he was just going to go and that he'd show us all. But he was a big bold kid of seventeen and said the white man's city didn't scare him much one way or the other. He'd stood up to those white teachers and didn't come to no harm, besides he was only going away long enough to make the money to buy a good piece of land to live and hunt on. Johnnie reckoned he'd be back in a year and asked me to go with him but I told him no I couldn't go because my brother Jack would have to come too and that would leave my mother all alone. I never told him that white men scared me right through just like my father who always said he didn't know whether he hated them more than he feared them or what. I used to see a look coming over his face when a white man from the government would come by our place and start asking questions about all kinds a things. You could feel the strength and hate gather together in him and get ready to jump right outside his skin and devour the man with the fat white face full of false teeth and shaving smells. The old man wouldn't lose that knot of hate and fear for days, probably not until he went into town and got so goddamned drunk that he'd break up the tavern and crack a few skulls before the cups clubbed him stupid and dragged him off to the jail. I had seen him drunk like that, his eyes swollen red with drink and blazing anger. He'd have his mouth torn wide open with screams in Indian I never understood. Jesus it took six men to hold still his twisting body while the cops clubbed him and put handcuffs on his wrists and ankles. Once when I was nine years old or thereabouts I tried to stop them and got smacked across the face so hard my mouth bled for two days. So I couldn't tell Johnnie how much a whole city full of white men terrified me and how they could make me feel like a hunted deer.

Besides I couldn't leave my mother like I said. She wasn't old but she was so sick that people would look at her extra long to see if they could see her soul trying to slip out of her body. She knew what they were thinking too and just tried to stand up straight like a birch sapling and prove them wrong. The doctor that came out to see her didn't seem to know his ass from a busted stovepipe and never told us nothing about her sickness, only gave her white man's medicines that never seemed to work. Jack and me just watched her die little by little every day. It was bad enough for me, but Jack had to watch her without saying a word because from the time he was about five he lost his words and never spoke. Sure he could smile and laugh and cry but he couldn't say nothin' to anybody even if he'd wanted. That's why he always did pretty much the same things that I done because I spoke for him and made sure that nobody took advantage of him. He was big enough to care for himself but he was sort of shy except when he played lacrosse. Then he'd get all worked up and wild looking just like the Old Man and it would take a dozen hard working priests to save the soul of any opponent he tangled with. By Christ he could be mean with his stick.

But Johnnie left all the same and Ed Kirk and David Whitewater went with him to Toronto to get rich enough to come back. All three of them gathered up their extra shirt and pair of pants and started to walk down to No. 7 to try to get a lift because they didn't have enough money for the bus. A bunch of us went with them down the rutted road and we talked about them comin' back with their pockets stuffed with $10 bills, enough to buy a new rifle and hunting dog and a piece of land somebody said. But Johnnie said he'd changed his mind already and he wanted to come back with a bus to form a bloody good Indian lacrosse team and travel all over the place playing the game for money. We would all become professionals and get rich that way. Rich enough so that we could live well on the Reserve and have a few dollars to buy whatever we wanted and maybe even get famous. We all laughed at the suggestion but kind of hoped it could come true even though none of us believed it was possible. Jesus! Just the thought of playing lacrosse for money and travelling around and meeting all those other teams make us want to get sticks and start practicing even though we knew that crazy Johnnie wouldn't be back home for at least a year. But it didn't matter, I felt like I was watching for the stars to fall again.

We left them at the highway, all of us waving every few minutes as we watched them disappear down the road with their sacks thrown over their wide shoulders. It was hard for those remaining because we had all known each other ever since we could remember. There just wasn't any new kids from the outside on the Reserve. There was just those you were born with. So when friends left, you lost brothers.

Loved

You are standing at the end of your driveway collecting the mail from you mailbox. You see your neighbour come out her front door, her little girl trailing behind her through the snow. She sees you and waves. You wave back, and she turns away, picks up her child, and hugs her very tightly. You know why. You know what she is thinking when she looks at you: the worst thing in the world can happen. You stand for a minute watching them get their car. You have a sudden desperate urge to run over and hop into the car with them, to spend the day holding the little girl's fat little hand and brushing her soft feathery hair out of her eyes. But of course you don't. Instead, you stand with your forehead pressed against the icy metal of your mailbox willing your brain to freeze into a solid chunk of ice.

This how fast a life unravels. You look at the clock on the wall above the counter near the fridge, and you are struck for a minute by how late it is. Already five-thirty, you say to yourself. You look out the window over the sink and see past the McConnell house, down to the road in between here and the lake. You feel a twinge of what—irritation? Frustration? A nagging feeling. She's late, you say. She should have been home a good half-hour ago. She's dawdling again, you tell yourself. She's such a dawdler. Always has been: staring off into space instead of doing up her shoelaces, staring at herself in the mirror instead of brushing her teeth.

You are tired today. You don't sleep well anymore. When she goes out you stay up half the night worrying about her getting home, and even when she stays home you worry about when she goes out. You wonder if she is drinking too much or having unprotected sex or doing drugs or meeting the wrong kind of boy, which is stupid because you know full well that the wrong kind of boy is the only kind you really want to meet, but you hope she hasn't met him yet and you remember Lee Miller. You pull the carrots out of the fridge and calculate that when you first met Lee you were exactly her age.

You finish peeling the carrots and put the water on to boil. You open the oven door and check the chicken. You lean against the counter for a minute trying to remember what you were going to do next. Turn down that TV, you yell down the hall to her brother, it's much too loud. I can hear it all the way in here. The television gets turned down marginally. You think again, what was I going to do? Oh yeah, you say, pour myself a drink. And you do. A gin and tonic. You even slice a bit of lemon. You lean against the stove and warm up your bum while you have your first sip, and it tastes so good. You tell yourself that you are so happy not to be an alcoholic so that you can enjoy this drink at the end of every day. Then you think maybe you are an alcoholic. After all, you really, really need this drink at the end of the day. Then you tell yourself that, if you wanted to, you could easily go without this drink. But then you tell yourself again how glad you are that since you are not an alcoholic you don't have to. Then you tell yourself out loud to stop it. Just stop it, you say.

You notice the water for the carrots is boiling, so you put the carrots in the pot and put the lid on. You peer out the back window again, almost pressing your face against the cold glass. Is that her? You squint. But it's not. Almost forty-five minutes late you think, but still you are not really worried. You just are not worried. By the time the chicken is done and the rice cooked and the table set and her father home you are a little worried, but actually, to be honest, you are more pissed off. Teenagers, you say to yourself, as you flip through the papers stuck to the fridge door trying to find Katie's number, trying to remember where she said she was going to be. Was it in fact Katie's? You walk down the hall and ask her brother if he has any idea where she went after school. He shrugs and doesn't take his eyes off of the insane music video he is watching. You stand in front of the TV and ask him again. How should I know? he says. You press on. Did he see her after school? Did he see her at school? You suddenly feel a wave of panic. Maybe she's been lost longer than you think. Lost? You feel a little shiver of fear start to creep up your back. But then your son says, yes, he did see her at school. He saw her standing out behind the gym, smoking. He watches your face for a second, waiting for you to get mad. You just say, okay thanks, to him and walk back down the hall to the kitchen and stare out the window again. You are so relieved that he saw her that you forget to be mad about the smoking. You have suspected her of smoking for a while now as her clothes have had a distinctly smoky smell lately, even though she always says that's just because the people she's with are smoking. Does she think you were born yesterday? You used to tell your mother the same thing. You go back to the fridge and locate Katie's number. You pick up the phone and dial. The line's busy. You hang up and look at the clock again and see that it is now almost seven o'clock. You stare out the back window and hope she was wearing a hat; it's freezing out. But then you remember watching her, the back of her getting smaller and smaller as she walked down the path away from the house, and you know she wasn't wearing her purple hat. You can see her hair caught up in a ponytail bobbing up and down as she walks.

(You never are able to find that hat anywhere in the house. You think maybe she had stuffed it in her bag. You tell yourself this every time you think about the purple hat but the truth is, like so many other details about that day, you will never know now.)

Pretty soon her brother walks down the hall wondering if he is ever going to eat, doesn't she know he's starving? You say, sit down, and you call her dad. You dish out the food, making a plate for yourself, which you will not eat. You carry your plate to the table. When you sit down your husband asks casually, where's C?

You have heard that when you are about to die your life flashes before your eyes. That is what happens to you. Only, it is her life that flashes before your eyes. Days and hours and minutes, all the scenes of her life, things that you didn't even know you remembered flash in rapid sequences across the movie screen of your mind. Her life unravels like a bolt of shockingly bright coloured fabric.

Anna

I'm in her living room, looking for her cat, when the phone rings. After five rings, the machine kicks in, and her voice rings out, "You've reached Anna, leave me a message." The sound of her voice makes me shiver and reminds me that I'm just on the better side of breaking and entering. I look at the front door to make sure she's not coming through it.

Then the message, "Anna? It's me, Michael. I need to speak to you. It's two o'clock on Saturday. Call me."

Me, Michael? That's a little goddamn familiar for a machine, I think. I immediately conjure images of Anna and Michael sitting on a park bench together, smiling and holding hands. The park bench is surrounded on all sides by yellow tulips.

I've been in the apartment for over four hours. Exploring. I filled a food bowl, but I haven't seen a cat. She'd said that his name was Moses and that he was all white with one black paw, like he'd dipped it in ink and was waiting to make his mark with it. Had she been lying?

I met Anna two months ago. I was having breakfast downtown when she walked in and took a table near me. She was beautiful and self-conscious. I ordered another coffee so that I could watch her eat and followed her out of the restaurant when she left. Her stride was a giveaway that she was used to having an audience. At the corner, I caught up to her and touched her on the arm. I told her that I'd followed her. That didn't surprise her, and she gave me a wary smile and told me her name.

Over the next few weeks we met regularly. I had sex with her once. I imagine myself married to her.

Then this week she told me that she would be out of town

for the weekend and that she needed me to feed her cat. She said that she didn't really know anyone else to ask, and would I mind? I'd only been to her place once before, briefly, and when she had excused herself to the bathroom, I had run to her bedroom, pulled back the bedcovers, and pushed my face into her pillows. No, I didn't mind.

And so it is that I am in her apartment, looking for a cat to justify my continued presence.

The floor is littered with books and magazines and newspapers. Judging by the proximity to the couch, she had recently been reading about the re-emergence of the Cathars, the fall of the Roman Empire, and the secrets of successful crop cultivating. All this for a proclaimed atheist who supports free enterprise and lives in an apartment.

The couch is long and covered in candy-green velvet. I imagine her in repose on it. I take off my shoes and lie down on the couch. I take off my shirt and my pants but stop at my socks and underwear. I walk into her bathroom and find her robe. It's full-length and purple. I put it on and look at myself in the mirror. The robe is straining at the shoulders, and it won't close around my body so there's a thick, solid strip of skin showing through, from head to foot. It doesn't escape me how strange this gesture is.

At this point the phone rings again. I return to the living room to hear her voice. And then it's Michael again. "Listen Anna, It's me again. I have something—"

I pick up, "Hello?"

He's flustered by my voice. "Yes? Hello? Is Anna there?

"No, she's not. She's out of town until tomorrow. I'm feeding Moses ... you know, the cat."

"I see," he says, "Listen, I really need to speak to her now. Do you know how I can reach her?"

"No. She didn't leave a number. I can pass on a message."

"I have some bad news. I'm a friend of Anna's, from Vancouver… I know this is a strange question, but please tell me honestly, do you know her well? Can I entrust you with something important to tell her?"

I'm standing in her robe and my white socks, and there is no way that I am going to be answering "no" to this question. "Yes, I know her well. We're involved," I blurt out with a rush.

"Fine. A friend of ours, someone Anna was close to, died this morning. His name was David."

I scream in my head and say, "My God, I'm sorry ... How did he die?"

"He died because he slit his throat."

I want to giggle at the solemnity with which he says this. It sounds like he's been rehearsing. "Oh ... Jesus," I exhale.

"Yes, I know."

Silence for a few beats, and then, "The funeral's in Vancouver on Tuesday."

"Was there a note? Will she know why?"

"No. There was no note, but maybe Anna will know."

Images start running through my mind. This dead man, David, is short, tall, beautiful, angry, fat, in a bathtub, outside, in a car, against a white background, a black background. His head is hardly attached, his throat is yawning, and there is blood spurting out of him. And he is afraid, and he is not afraid, and then choking. And she will care, and she will care a lot. She will cry, and she will think of him in wishful and tragic ways, especially on his birthday and when she has simple perfect nostalgia for her childhood years.

"What did he look like?" I ask.

"What?"

"I'm sorry, but I want to know," I tell him.

Michael pauses and says, "He was pale. He had white skin, and he had red, red lips. And light blue eyes. He was sort of delicate."

He stops again. "Listen, I'm sorry to bring you into this, but it's better that she hear it from you, than from a machine. Thank you."

I hang up.

Now there is a male Snow White in the room. He's delicate and tragic and dead. I realize that I'm furious that she has this tale of tragedy and that it in no way includes me.

I take off what I am wearing, and I get into her bed. I lie on my back, as still as possible, and I pull the sheets up to my chin. I think of what I'll say to her, "David is dead. He cut his throat." And as she crumples, I'll say, "But I won't cut my throat, honey. I don't like the feel of pain, honey"—like the little brother who doesn't understand romance.

I realize that she is a stranger. And I'm a stranger who will come up to her and touch her on and the arm and whisper softly that this David is dead. I'll rip apart the fabric of context and tell her something that has meaning, that has reverb and resonance. But Snow White has already been cast in this drama, there's no part big enough for me. I get out of the bed and put my clothes back on. I hang up her robe, smooth her sheets, and leave quietly.

Dumpster

Clank!

"Well you know what? Fuck her. Anyone who gives you this much grief belongs out of your life." Nick washed down his words with another swig of his forty. Labatt Wildcat, 8%.

"Yeah, well, whatever man. Belong or not, she's gone," Chris looked up from his wet sneakers. Half-snow, half-rain started to fall, spotting the dark pavement darker. The boys shivered and looked at each other.

"Another one?" Nick asked. They raised their oversized bottles and, without a toast, knocked them together. *Clank!* The mouths of their bottles pressed to their blue lips, the beer sliding down their throats easily. They felt it splash somewhere deep inside. Nick suddenly pulled his bottle away and coughed out an arcing booze spit on the alley wall.

"Easy there. You okay?"

"Yeah yeah, I'm fine. Let's go."

Chris threw his empty bottle down the lane and watched it explode like a dull firework, the shards spattering the asphalt and brick. They turned and walked in the opposite direction, down Greene Avenue then onto Ste-Catherine Street. A yellow public-security car slowed past. Chris made eye contact with the driver, tightened his stare, glaring. The car sped off.

The depanneur door chimed as they entered. White light flooded their vision.

"Back so soon, guys? Not another one already?" Mrs. Kim beamed at them from behind the crowded counter of lollipops, postcards, and scratch tickets. The boys rubbed their eyes and headed for the fridge, grabbing two more.

"You know, I should really ask for some ID, I could get in trouble," Mrs. Kim said through a compassionate smile, the skin constricting around her eyes.

"Come on Mrs. Kim, we're eighteen," Chris countered, incredulous. "We buy here all the time!"

"Yeah, who gives you more business than us? We can just as easily buy down the street," Nick offered.

"Okay okay. But next time bring ID."

"Sure thing," Chris said, smug as he smoothed out a twenty from a crumpled ball produced from a pocket.

They walked out of the dep holding bottles by the neck, the brown paper bag crinkled under their grip. Security drove by again. This time Chris kept his eyes fixed on the sidewalk. They walked back to the alley as the drizzle turned into fine mist. The bricks absorbed the moisture like tear stained cheeks. Chris twisted open his beer first, then Nick. *Clank!* They lit up smokes from the same pack, Nick's pack, and tried to think of something to say.

"I can't believe the game last night."

"I missed it."

"They came out flying, three goals in the first period. The Leafs' only good scoring chance was a Mogilny breakaway, and Theo stoned him. But things fell apart in the second. They lost their edge, and Toronto took over. 5-3 final."

"Yeah, I saw the paper. They do this every year, get my hopes up. Flashes of brilliance, but they can't sustain it. I can't watch anymore."

The rain stopped just as the yellow security car pulled up. Nick swore, and Chris started chugging. The guard approached them. Full lips and large round eyes, translucent somehow, like brown glass.

"How many times do we have to do this? You know you're not supposed to be here." The security guard's tone was more older brother than law enforcer.

"Ibrahim, you're right," Chris was quick to respond, an eager smile now on his face. "We're totally outta here. Sorry, man."

"Alright. But seriously, guys, one more time, and I'm pouring out your beer and giving you both a ticket."

"Ibrahim, we're gone. You never saw us. We love you."

Ibrahim sighed and shook his head as Nick and Chris screwed the caps back on their bottles and walked back onto Greene. The boys walked west along Ste-Catherine, looking for a suitable drinking spot.

"Someplace with a roof. The rain's starting again, if it really gets going I don't want to get soaked."

"How about there?" Chris pointed at a house on the corner. It had been partly renovated, only the front red-brick facade and part of the roof remained. The rest was just a skeleton of support beams and temporary plywood floors. It had been gutted. The new roof was half-built, it did not have tiles yet, and there were gaps in the pale wood that faced the sky.

"Perfect."

On the second floor they sat on a bouncy piece of plywood. The rain fell steadily a few feet away, through a gap in the roof and right down into the basement. Standing, unsteady, the boys walked the straight line to the back of the house, the floor missing on either side of them.

"Time for another?"

"Let's do it," Nick said. "It's cool that security let us keep our beer. That other guy always pours it out right in front of us."

"Hassan."

"What?"

"The other guy. His name is Hassan," said Chris.

"Christ, how do remember these guys' names?"

"It's a disease, I remember everything," Chris said, looking at the yard below, at the dumpster and the mud.

"How do we get down?" Nick asked.

"How the fuck did we get up?" They looked at each other in confusion, then looked around the second floor. There must have been a ladder, but they couldn't see any ladder. How could they have gotten up without a ladder? There were no stairs.

"Well shit, we didn't fly up here. You're the guy who remembers everything, you tell me."

They sat at the edge of the house, legs dangling off the side. They smoked.

"I guess we'll have to jump."

"I'm not going to jump off the second storey of a house. We'll hurt ourselves."

"I got it. We'll jump into the dumpster. The trash'll be soft," Nick said, excited by his idea.

"Into the trash? Gross, man."

"Well, unless you find that ladder there isn't a better way."

Resigned, Chris agreed. Both refusing to go first, they resolved to go at the same time. Crouched down, backs to the yard, they eased themselves off the side of the wall, holding onto the floor for support. Hanging by their fingertips, their bodies outstretched, Nick counted off *1-2-3*, and they let themselves go.

The trash wasn't soft domestic trash. There were no garbage bags filled with dirty Kleenex, drained milk cartons, and empty chip bags. The dumpster was filled with construction waste. Chunks of broken brick wall, torn away Gyprock, and splintered wood all mixed together in an industrial salad.

"You fucking idiot. I fucking hate you, man."

"How was I supposed to know! Are you okay? I think I'm okay. Are you okay?"

"I think there's a nail in my leg."

"Does it hurt?"

"Not really. It feels weird. But it doesn't hurt."

They slowly climbed out of the dumpster, climbing the steel wall and dropping to the safety of the ground. Scraped and a little bruised, clothing ripped in places, they inspected each other's damage. Chris pulled up his pant leg to reveal where the nail had been. Already the blood had coagulated, the nail hadn't gone deep.

"One more?" Chris asked.

"Yeah, one more. You okay with that leg? Shouldn't you get a booster shot or something?"

"I think. What's a booster shot, though?"

"I dunno, really. Just when you cut yourself on metal you're supposed to get one."

"Tomorrow. I'll do it tomorrow. Right now, let's get one more."

"Cool."

Katharine O'Flynn

Summer's End

That summer, as always, Glenda went to the farm, to stay with Gram
and Baxter and Lou. Theirs was an old-fashioned farm, with horses
instead of tractors, on account of Gram and Baxter's religion.

Glenda's sisters wouldn't go, not if you paid them, they said.
Nothing to do there. Nobody to hang around with.

But Glenda liked the farm.

She had her own special place to play: a cave-like opening in the
cedar hedge. She liked it that she could play games that she was almost
too old for, and that her sisters weren't there to boss her and to make
up new rules and start fights. She could talk to herself and nobody
listened to make fun of her.

She made dolls from hollyhock flowers, and furniture from burrs.
She played farm with herds of pebble animals—little white sheep
and pigs, and bigger pinks, greys and blacks for horses and cows.
She arranged treasures she'd found: bits of cracked china, old medi-
cine bottles of coloured glass, a blue coffee pot with a leak, rusted
bolts. Every autumn she buried these treasures and drew a map with
an X to mark the hiding place so she could find them again the next
summer. It pleased her that the treasures were always there waiting
for her to rediscover.

When she was tired of playing, she would follow Baxter and
Lou around while they worked. She liked evening chores best. Lou
milked and Baxter fed the animals and Glenda helped, running back
and forth from the warmth of the dusty, straw-smelling stable into
the cool green twilight.

Baxter hardly ever spoke except to give commands: "Hand me
that lad, would you?" or "Take these lads and set them on the chop
box." He called everything lads.

Lou had such a terrible stammer that he didn't like to talk at all. He wouldn't even answer questions except to point or nod or shrug.

It was quiet in the stable except for small contented sounds: pigs snuffing up chop with little grunts; cows' tails swish-swishing; the cats' tongues clicking as they lapped milk from their old pie-plate dish.

After evening chores, Gram and Baxter and Lou sat together around the kitchen stove, or out on the stoop when the weather was warm, just sitting, not needing to talk or argue or watch TV like her mother and stepfather at home in the city.

Maybe it was so Lou wouldn't need to feel different and ashamed that Baxter and Gram didn't talk much, Glenda thought

Sundays Glenda's mother telephoned. "Are you alright? Are you sure you want to stay? You could come home and do summer playground with Cindy and Becca. They're taking swimming lessons."

Glenda didn't want to be herded with a bunch of noisy kids into a cold, white-tiled pool where shouts echoed and water got up your nose and made you think you were drowning.

"No."

"You're not lonely? You do understand why we can't visit you there?"

"Yes."

It was because of the divorce. Gram and Baxter and Lou were her Dad's family, though Glenda wasn't sure how they fitted together. Gram must be her Dad's mother, but was Baxter his father? If he was, why didn't they call him Grandad? And Lou? He was too old to be a cousin, so he was probably an uncle.

She was too shy to ask. Maybe she was supposed to know the connections. Maybe they were secrets.

It wasn't like her mum's family. She knew exactly who everyone of them was: Granny and Gramps and aunts and uncles and cousins were all accounted for and each one had a place in the family stories.

In this family, they didn't tell stories, or not out loud, anyway.

But Glenda liked her farm family. She felt at home in their silent circle. "I'd like to stay here always, like Lou," she said.

"Lou doesn't always find it to his liking here," Gram said sharply. "You'll want to go too before long."

At hay-cutting time, Glenda rode on the mower with Baxter. She leaned against him, his arms and the reins encircling her. As the square of uncut hay grew smaller with each round, she told herself stories about the groundhogs and rabbits and kildeer that lived there and their plans to avoid destruction. In her stories, they always escaped, but only at the last minute.

Once she wanted to ride with Lou when he did the raking, but Baxter said, "No. You stay by me."

When they drew in the hay, she stood beside Baxter on the wagon. He drove the team, and Lou built the loads. As they turned into the barnyard with a full load, Lou would slide off with his fork. Then Baxter turned the team up the gangway and shook the reins and shouted "Hurrah, lads!" and Lou would whack the off-horse with the blunt side of the fork and make a strange shout and the startled horses would strain up the slope and thunder into the barn.

Baxter told her it didn't hurt the horse, only encouraged him to behave right.

One day when Glenda was playing at her place in the hedge, she looked up and saw Lou staring at her, open-mouthed with a sad, strange look, and she knew right then what Gram meant when she'd said Lou didn't always find the farm to his liking. It was scary and it wasn't right, the way he was looking at her.

Luckily Baxter came along just then. "Get on out of there," he shouted to Lou and whacked him with the back of the shovel he was carrying, the same way Lou whacked the horse on the gangway.

"You alright?" Baxter asked her.

"Yeah."

"Lou sneaks up on you anytime like that, you fetch me or Gram right away, you hear?"

"Yeah." She wondered again who Lou was—a man who wouldn't speak, a man that Baxter could hit like an animal to make him behave. This wasn't right either.

The grain ripened in the fields. Every morning now, on the way back from driving the milk cows to the south pasture, Baxter would take a stalk of oats and pull off the bearded kernels, running them between his fingers while he looked out over the golden field.

One morning he said, "We'll reap these lads today."

Glenda sat beside him on the binder and watched the heavy grain bend and fall and drop to the stubbled ground in neat bundles. She told herself her stories about the frightened birds and rabbits and mice of the field. She whispered warnings to them to run from the false shelter of the standing grain. "Run towards the cleared land," she urged. "Run into the open." They must have listened, for on the last sweep no creatures were caught cowering, waiting for the blade.

On the last day of summer, Glenda buried her treasures as usual in the cedar hedge. This time, though, she made no map. By next year she might have forgotten where they were. But it wouldn't matter, because she knew that, really, they weren't treasures at all.

Red Suitcases

"This trip is going to work out, sweetie," Guy says. "Just what we've been waiting for. A happy ending."

I sigh. During the four years we've been trying to get pregnant, I've come to hate Christmas. I loathe Christmas travel even more, but at least we miss le réveillon and the Boxing Day rituals, all our nieces and nephews plunging into their presents.

We are standing in The Bay's luggage section during the pre-Christmas rush, not a salesperson in sight. By the doorway, a snowy bicycle courier is considering the boxes of chocolates. He lingers over the After Eights but finally selects a bar of Toblerone. It's a good choice for a sister. But perhaps they're for his mother? Immediately, my eyes moisten.

Even the suitcases come in families, I think. Large, medium, and small, sorted by manufacturer. A flash of red orients me like a compass needle to the Air Canada label, while Guy targets the Samsonite next door, oblivious to the sombre greys and blacks.

I can't help noticing that a valise across the aisle comes in a perky pink, which I could sling over my shoulder on my way to the delivery room. Month after month, I've visualized the scene: breathing with difficulty, I'd dial Guy's cell. No answer—he'd be patiently dealing with customers. I'd leave a message punctuated with labour pains and call a cab to St. Mary's, the pre-packed valise at my feet.

"They only sell them in red at Christmas," a salesperson offers, disturbing my reverie. "Stands out on the carousel, one of our most popular lines."

"Lucky," I say. We're flying to Beijing in a party of eight couples and two singles, and we'll need the visual aid when we navigate the transfers in Tokyo. Then I remember, from my course in interior design last spring, how followers of Feng Shui believe red *is* a lucky colour, full of sun-rising energy, and happiness.

The salesperson is pulling out an extension handle when Guy approaches us. "We'll have our hands full coming back from China, won't we, sweetheart?"

He examines the front zippered pockets and spins the wheels in turn. He glances over at the woman, and her eyes widen a smidgen. Given the chance, he'll proudly announce we're adopting an infant next week.

"Let's take two," I say quickly.

The salesperson trails the pair behind her in a path to the cash register that prevents another marooned couple from soliciting her attention. I wonder if she would have congratulated us.

I abandon Guy on the sidewalk with the suitcases while I fetch the car. Montreal in the December twilight brings on even darker reflections. Everyone has a separate journey, I think. No-one understands each other; even my husband is an unreachable star.

"Relax," Guy says as I honk the car ahead. "You're going to be a great—"

"Don't say it!"

"You'll see."

Silent, I drive into our driveway. Two Christmases ago, I'd tumbled bikinis and books into a packsack, convinced Guy and I simply needed a Caribbean backdrop to conceive. Last January we'd gone skiing at Mont Tremblant. In six days, we'll fly over a continent and an ocean, our new luggage held up in the stratosphere by a force unfathomable to me.

On the nursery floor, Guy is crouching to unzip each suitcase. He places them on their sides so that the covers flop to the floor, and the image I've been trying to suppress all week pops into my head. An open suitcase reveals a lifeless woman. Naked and contorted, her limbs are folded so that all the available space contains her. It's a true story. Last week, I'd read in the paper, a Mexican smuggled herself into Vancouver International Airport, her future extinguished in the suitcase she flew in. It became her coffin.

"Rose, are you alright?"

I nod and pick up the list our adoption agency sent. There are two columns, one for each suitcase, and space to tick off each item. "Diapers," I intone. "His and hers."

Guy hunts among the bundles on the floor and stows a dozen inside each suitcase.

"Three sizes of nipples," I continue, the words stumbling on my tongue. "Hers."

Soon calamity sets in. His suitcase—lice comb. Check. Her suitcase—rectal thermometer. Check.

The next day, Guy braves a snowstorm to purchase objects we'd forgotten, some Zincofax and Ihle's Paste for skin irritations. I photocopy our master file for the Chinese authorities before confirming the brand of floor tiles to renovate a client's kitchen. My flat stomach belies our intentions, and I've come to appreciate the anonymity. I simply tell my clientele that, yes, we are closed over the holidays; we might take a last-minute trip.

On an impulse, Guy detours to Ikea and brings home cups for the baby to stack in all the colours of the rainbow. Later, we pose for official photographs, unsmiling. Before we know it, the week is up.

The night before we fly, I startle awake, suspended in a bubble, which I recognize as the shape of fear. Barefoot, I glide across the landing to the nursery. The open curtains reveal a luminous moon over a fir tree, the picture of a cozy Christmas if our neighbour's lights were on, but their house is dark, like ours. The night is windless; nevertheless, the gripping cold of the Montreal winter presses in. The backyard, already impassably deep in snow, makes it hard to remember we've grown vegetables there.

Inside, the nursery is immaculate, and waiting. Crib, changing table, and armoire: everything is here. Yet it is the open suitcases that command my attention. In Guy's suitcase reside the photostatic prints of our birth records, and in mine rests a copy of our wedding certificate. We are legitimate parents-to-be, so why do I feel like an impostor?

Gently, I dislodge key documentation from the folds of a yellow quilt inside my suitcase. It is our notarized adoption order from the Québec Court. I seat myself gingerly in the rocking chair and recall how the judge stared hard at me. His first question took me aback.

"Are you ready?"

Was I? Guilt suffused me then. It still does. I'm not ready. I'll never be ready.

My heart feels immobilized and weighted as the suitcases in front of me. I consider my options. Return them to The Bay, a dissatisfied customer. Desert them on the luggage carousel. Omit this official paper with its seal. Never get on the plane. With each possibility, I feel lighter, almost giddy. Mother Nature won't be throwing the dice, not this time.

In the moonlight, my grief—for the baby I'll never give birth to—shrinks and flattens, until it becomes a layer so thin it could line the bottom of a drawer, or fold inside a suitcase so lightly, you'd hardly know it was there.

Flying Home

Papa Bill he ran off down 8th, he was always late, jumped the shuttle at 42nd over to Grand Central. Down down down and lost in himself and the notes of the busker at the bottom of the stairs, he flashed panic once when he snapped back into time, catching sight of the number 6 heading uptown, thinking he's on the wrong platform, shuffling his impatient foot on the wrong floor, leaning against the wrong wall.

No, he realized with a sigh set free by relief, he was going downtown, he was on track.

When the number 6 finally pulled up he squeezed in among the rest of the flow to lean and hold the post in front of him. As the train drew south he watched the lights on the line map close one by one like sleepy eyes.

"You know, Cap" (he'd been calling me Cap about two years, since I turned twelve; until then, it'd been Captain), "I'll tell you how I once saw it."

He took a long drag on his cigarette, stared up at the kitchen light, leaned back in his chair, and blew smoke straight and hard like he was trying to blow out the light bulb itself. He'd just finished eating. My mom was always happy to see him, said he could come by any time he wanted, there would be enough for him. They'd been friends since long before I was born. He used our couch more than once between gigs. He'd been around forever, like an uncle.

28th Street and the doors of the car slowed open, his pace wide, the extra weight he was carrying casting his stride slightly uneven. With his left index finger he quickly traced the "2" in the "28" tiled into the wall, those tiles placed here one by one by an unknown hand many years before him, and passed it in less than a breath. His right hand grasped the handle of a shadowblack case, brushed aluminum lips clasping together the two shadowy halves, holding inside the wear-tarnished brass he made seem flow like good gold beer on a summer's afternoon.

"I was sitting in the park on a beautiful June day, warm but new like spring, and thought about finally learning to read music. I closed my eyes under the trees near the water next to Camel Rock" (a name I'd given it—we used to walk there together) "and imagined myself facing a staff, just like you see it on the page. I placed a few dots on the lines and in the spaces and named them.

"Then something fun began happening. I started floating slowly towards the staff, it getting bigger as I got closer. I went through the bars—I was as big as the notes themselves—and saw it from the other side. It was just this suggestion in space, hanging there in a silent white background, the notes like pores in the skin of silence."

He surfaced, and the concrete under his feet sent him south on Park to 27th and left to Lexington. Down the street he saw the name on the canopy, guessed he wasn't *too* late and pulled open the glass door. On his right layered up the wall he nodded to the black and whites of the greats, framed and preserved from the eclipse of time by each passing eye. The foyer a lush red, a matte black door with a simple four-letter neon word glowing above it—JAZZ.

He inhaled his way downstairs, the door brushing quietly closed behind him. The bartender nodded hello, raising his eyebrows and shaking a percussive martini.

"I stared at the staff awhile from the other side, then came back to it. This time, I stayed on the staff and found myself sitting there *inside the note* like I was inside a bubble. Next thing, I'm moving along the staff, bouncing up and down the lines and spaces through the music playing my heart."

He paused, and looked over at me.

"That's when I knew where I lived."

He took one long last drag on his smoke, butted it, and exhaled as he stretched his arms behind his head, locking his fingers and gazing again at the kitchen light.

"I opened my eyes. I was lying flat on my back, looking up through the leaves and into the blue. Man, I could've fallen into the sky."

Backstage, Paul, Evan, and Sam were waiting, their usual composed selves. He wet the reed as their name was announced, went through the door and onto the stage.

After a quick silence of exchanged glances, they conjured the opening notes and Papa Bill was gone, blue and flying.

Vandals in Sandals

"Can't we open the windows? I'd like to hear the leaves."

"Air conditioning. Better to keep them shut."

Max was still annoyed with Bea for having clipped the wing mirror on the way out of the garage. The mirror hung limply, broken at the bone. Bea felt bad about it, since the van was new. She looked out at the poplar leaves spinning on their stems. She knew without hearing them that the lush sound of well-waxed summer leaves had been replaced with a clattering like rice wafers. Fall was coming and, after that, nothing but snow. Cammy's little brown hand from the backseat appeared with an apple core.

"You can throw it out the window here, sweetie," Bea said. "It's the country."

"Don't encourage her to litter, Bea. It's all someone's frontage."

Bea looked at the maple seedlings and the crooked fence and the darkness of the firs behind.

"Okay. Give it to me, Cammy. I'll save it for the compost. Where's the trash container?"

"Here." Max pressed a button and a compartment slid open. "Don't forget to get it out later," he said.

"Are we there yet?"

"No, we're still looking. The agent said it was around here somewhere." Bea looked at the map again. "So we've passed Lac Vert, right?"

"Not sure. Thought you were doing the map."

Oh, give it up, she thought. Get a grip. It's only the wing mirror. She looked out the window again. The road curved past a stand of beeches. The layered quality of their branches seemed familiar, like hands outspread, pleading for calm.

"Slow down, I think the turnoff's back there, after the beeches. Before the dumpsters."

"Are you sure?"

"Yes, I'm sure."

Max made a U-turn, and they drove back past three dumpsters overflowing with Labour Day discards. A tilting pile of tires leaned into the ragweed. Nearby, a useless sled lay in the sun, its slats curled up in a snarl.

"Look, a sled," said Cammy. "Can I have it?"

"It's trash," said her father.

"But I could fix it."

"Look we don't have time to pick up trash for you as well as for your mother."

"Sorry, Daddy."

"Don't worry, love," said Bea. "If we find a cottage to buy we'll get you a new sled for the winter. How about that?"

The van started up the hill. With a click all the doors locked. Bea didn't like it. The van was just too much. The roadside was bright with black-eyed susans, some pure yellow and fine as stars, others rusty as old nails. Day lilies had seeded in the ditches, and tendrils of purple vetch fingered over the greenery. They sped past a swampy area spiked with dead trees. A nerve in Bea's jaw tingled with recognition; she knew this road, she knew these trees. Once upon a time a boy called Yves had shown her a heron perched high on a skeletal branch in this very swamp. Bea had been ten, spending the summer in a rented cottage with her parents.

Yves lived in the neighbouring cottage. Together, the children explored the jewel box of the land. Once he plucked at her sleeve to draw her attention to a young fox chasing flies on the path in front of them. Bea thought that nothing could equal the fox, but she was the first to see the weasel slipping along under the rock fall, its dark body undulating like an animated moustache. One afternoon they watched a pair of catfish herding their young about in the shallows. Yves made gestures indicating that the parents ate their babies. Bea watched the tiny wriggling commas with renewed interest. Another day she showed him a snake, run over and flat as a shoelace. The next, Yves showed her a discarded shoelace, flat and braided as a squashed snake.

Inside the cottage Bea's parents played cards by lamplight and went to bed early. The lamps emitted a soft ball of light, not bright enough to do anything by, except, as she realized now, conceive a second child. Each morning Bea washed the shadow of soot out of the glass chimneys. At the end of the summer they beat out carpets, took down flypapers, pulled the curtains, and drove one last time down the bumpy driveway. Bea saw Yves out the back window. Small, he waved from the dock.

The day of the heron they had been heading out to swim in the lake at the bottom of the hill, but when Yves reached the end of the driveway he turned and ran uphill instead, shouting for Bea to follow. Just when she thought that she could run no more, Yves started back down the hill into the dip where the swamp pressed close to the sides of the road. Hot and sweating they passed into a band of water-cooled air, entering a chilled land, where ghosts dwelt in the sunlight. The yellow daisies shone like stars beside the road and the heron rose up in flight. Yves and Bea flapped their arms and ran on down to swim. She kept her T-shirt on. His strong brown legs glistened when he came out of the water, wet like a salamander.

Now the road had been sealed. The daylilies still filled the ditches, although Hydro workers had cut the tops off the pines to make way for the cables. Max kept driving, but the road ended in a cliff face. Bea knew that. She had climbed there with Yves, searching for fossils.

Bea had to put her glasses on to read the words spray-painted onto the rock. She flushed and looked at the map. *Petit Hibou, ça m'empêche pas de continuer à t'aimer. Yves.*

"Funny name for a girl," said Max. "Old Yves sounds a bit desperate. It's quite the custom round here to proclaim your love on a rock. Remember all those names on the way up to La Tuque?"

"What does it say, daddy?"

"It says that he won't stop loving her. Little vandal."

"What's a vandal?"

"A person who wears sandals and writes on walls."

"Vandals in sandals."

"Yes, and Goths in socks."

"Vandals in sandals and Goths in socks, Goths in thocks. Thocks in Goths."

"Do you think we could open a window *now*?" Bea's voice was sharp. The brittle sound of the late summer leaves came to her. The locusts roared in the banks.

"Looks like this is a dead end," said her husband. "I guess your hunch was wrong."

"I guess it was, I'm sorry," she said.

"No problemo, it's a nice day to be out for a drive, isn't it, Cammy? In our sandals in the new vandal."

"Vandal sandal candle dandle." Cammy launched into the rest of the alphabet. The words fell like light blows. The mother endured them all. Surely, she thought, it can't always be like this. They turned and drove back down the hill, past the swamp, past the empty branch where the heron had been, past the daisies, and back to the dumpsters at the bottom of the road.

The Assignment

—Surely, Jed, a bright lad like yourself could have written *something*.

(Is he being sarcastic? He must know my grades are way down this year.)

—Honest, sir, I tried.

—And?

—Nothing came to mind.

(Mr. Gordon rolls his eyes—his signal that he would allow the class a few snickers. Yeah, there were snickers.)

—Impossible, my boy! Things are happening all around you. Think! Remember! Write!

(Mr. G waves me to my seat and adds,)

—Jed, I'll settle for one good page, on my desk first thing in the morning. Otherwise...

(I know his "otherwise" ... hell and damn! Now Jordan, the self-anointed class clown, raises his hand.)

—Please, sir, a suggestion. Maybe he could start it, "One dark and stormy night..."

(More snickers, the idiots!)

—Not bad, Jordan!

(Teach playing to the crowd; finally, the screeching bell.)

In the library, I open my loose-leaf. I think! Oh yeah, I remember! Okay. Why not? I start to write.

TITLE: ONE DARK AND STORMY NIGHT

One dark and stormy night, this time last year, my father tried to kill my ma.

(Good start, Mr. G? A punchy opening?)

He pushed her down the cellar stairs. She said she fell.

But I saw what happened.

The storm woke me--flashes of lightning, heavy winds, thunderclaps right above the house. Then a real big one. I tried my lamp. Nothing. I heard some crashing. It seemed like inside. Did something break loose?

(Something did, alright!)

Then there were three or four flashes in a row and thunder so loud I could feel it. I made my way downstairs. In the next flash, I saw them.

It looked at first like they were hugging. Had she come down, fallen, been scared? I moved forward. Then I saw him give her a push and quickly catch her towards him by the shoulders. Another push away ... what? ... he was shaking her, damn it! I couldn't hear anything except the storm.

"Dad, stop!" I yelled. He turned. She loosened one arm. In the quick bursts of light, their faces looked twisted, unreal. "Stay away, kid!" he snarled. "Your ma..." He caught her free arm. I don't know what he was going to say because I lunged and grabbed him--"Go, Ma!"-- and tried to hold on. He's bigger than me and used to wrestle. He stank of liquor. He gave a kind of growl, lifted me up, and threw me a few feet down the hall. My head hit a table.

I saw my ma run and fall over something. He dragged her over to the cellar stairs. She screamed. "No, Ed, no!" Her cries were cut off by the explosions outside. "Damn you, that's the last time..." his words got lost, too. He pushed her hard. I saw that. Then I must have blacked out.

At the hospital she told her story (with my father standing near her, I'm sure). They believed her. They always do. By morning, the storm ended. It had caused a lot of damage. Then people put things back together. The fallen tree branches were easy. The rest? I don't know.

THE END

(Is that enough, Mr. G?)

Allons Enfants de la Patrie

Lucy and Deb were the dykes who lived above the sex shop. They were falling apart. After they'd gone weeks without making love, Deb said to Lucy, "Something's wrong with our relationship; we just don't realize it yet." Lucy just shrugged and turned over.

That night they heard strange noises outside. Lucy got up and went to look out the window. She peered down, then said, "They're moving stuff into Richard's office." She paused, peering again. "It looks like ... massage tables." Deb got up and looked too. Sure enough, some guys were moving upholstered tables into the second-floor apartment.

The sex shop was on street level, and Deb and Lucy were on the third floor, in a big, sunny, cheap old apartment. Sandwiched in between them and the vinyl dresses and cherry-flavoured lube was the second-floor apartment their landlord used as his office. God knew what he did down there, in seven-and-a-half rooms—once, they'd seen him waltzing drunkenly on the deck below with the statue of a naked woman. Their apartment had an inside staircase from the second floor, which meant that their front door and his were next to each other, but they slipped their rent cheques through the mail slot of the shop, so they didn't see much of him.

Weeks is a long time to go without sex when you're in bed together every night, but at first they hadn't paid attention. They were both busy, sleep-deprived. Plus, Lucy's uptight mother had visited over the February break with Lucy's young brother. She was so uncomfortable with Lucy's lesbianism, she'd only reluctantly agreed to stay. There would definitely be no sex while she was around. She showed her disapproval in weird ways—criticizing the furniture, the food. She came home one day with a pile of flat white-paper parcels of expensive meat—roast beef, prosciutto—from the little French butcher shop Deb and Lucy always avoided because the guy was such a creep. Lucy's mum raved about this store, its shelves laden with jars of imported baby carrots and spring peas, implying that it showed her superiority that she shopped there (and their inferiority that they didn't). Lucy almost lost it; she'd left the apartment, seeking temporary refuge at her best friend Jen's place. The next day, her mother suddenly announced that she couldn't allow her son to be exposed to "immorality" anymore, and within an hour they were gone, a week early—leaving the little white-wrapped parcels stacked neatly in the fridge. Lucy missed her brother terribly and cried all day.

After that, Lucy and Deb just never got back to having sex. They were too tired, or it was too late, or Lucy was out with Jen, or ... or she just didn't feel like it. There was no arguing with that. Deb ended up feeling, obscurely, that it was her fault—so she tried harder. She made Lucy chicken pot pies from scratch. She did Lucy's laundry. She didn't complain when they decided to see a movie and Lucy rode her bike, even though she knew Deb couldn't ride with her because of her bad knees. Deb kept thinking Lucy would get over it, because Lucy *said* she still loved her.

Except for lack of sex, their routine stayed about the same; downstairs, however, everything had changed. Their first clue came the day after the surreptitious move-in. That afternoon they suddenly heard it: loud and clear, the first notes of "La Marseillaise." They looked at each other. They heard the muffled sound of footsteps and then the downstairs door opening. The massage place seemed to have installed a new doorbell, which played the opening bars of the French national anthem. Very soon they became intimately familiar with that tune—and they began to realize what, exactly, was going on.

For some reason, although there was a lot of traffic in and out— the doorbell sounding its fluty notes relentlessly from mid-morning until late night, doors opening and closing, the distant thrum of voices—the only place they ever heard really intrusive noise was in their kitchen. The first time, they were having dinner with friends when suddenly they heard the unmistakable accelerating complaint of a massage table being subjected to a use for which it had not been designed. Everyone paused, forks in hand; even their jaws froze in mid-chew as they looked at each other, wide-eyed. (Afterward, Lucy gleefully imitated the sound to everyone they knew, squeaking maniacally.)

Over the next several weeks their relationship continued to quietly disintegrate, to the accompaniment of the stirring strains of "La Marseillaise." The more sex was being had on the massage tables below, the further it receded from the bed upstairs. Now and then their doorbell would buzz and a man would be standing in the doorway, asking "Est-ce que Chantal (or Giselle, or Cindy) est là?" Lucy and Deb couldn't imagine what the men thought, looking at them with their brushcut hair, their faces clear of makeup, Lucy's mountain bike hanging from a hook over the stairs. It got to the point where they'd jerk their thumbs towards the other door before the men could even open their mouths.

It ended as suddenly as it had begun. One night as Lucy and Deb lay stiff in bed in the dark, they heard shuffling and thumping on the stairs. Lucy looked out the window and reported that the massage tables were being moved out. The next day the doorbell was quiet. It rang again occasionally; once Deb got home from work and Lucy told her the police had been by—a few days too late. After that it was just stragglers, johns with the old classified ad still folded, smudged, in their wallets.

Finally in April, Lucy announced she was leaving to spend the summer treeplanting with Jen. She said she needed the money, she wanted to get out of the city, she and Jen wanted to spend more time together ... Deb put her face in her hands. How could Lucy have made plans to go away for three months without consulting her?

How could Lucy leave her alone for so long? Wait a minute—Deb looked up—she was leaving to spend the summer *with Jen*?

Their screaming fight ended with Deb choked with anguish and mucus, barely able to talk; Lucy stormed off, toothbrush and change of clothes stuffed into her knapsack, vowing to move out by the end of the month. After Lucy had slammed the door, Deb sank, unmoving, to the bottom step, tears welling from her reddened eyes. Night fell, and the staircase grew dark, but Deb still sat, paralyzed. Hours later, when the buzzer went, she only had to stand and step forward to open the door, hope fighting humiliated anger at the thought that it might be Lucy returning. But it wasn't; it was the butcher from the shop down the street, the folds of his meaty jowls hanging sadly against his red neck, his watery blue eyes peering timidly from his face.

"Est-ce que Chantal est là?" he asked.

Europa

Myles Fish sits hunched at the kitchen table, watching his hand twitch and dance inches away from the white plastic pill-keeper. When the shaking stops he can take his medication, but there will be only the briefest of opportunities. He must be diligent.

"Listen!" A muffled voice from the living room, over the ostinato of television: "They're shooting tear gas at the protestors—why?"

"Tears shut people up," Myles says. He knows Kate cannot hear him through the tinny chanting, the sound of falling pickets hitting pavement, the popping of canisters, the cultivated concern (head ducking slightly sideways, eyes grave, left hand gripping the mike) of the on-location reporter. Kate's comments from the couch have more to do with placing a husband, like furniture, in her circumscribed world. This is their agreement: she includes him in her CNN soliloquies as if he were there, he responds from his chair in the kitchen as if she could hear. Myles completely misses Kate's next outburst: "Ohmygod. It's beautiful!"

In that moment Myles's world is turning.

He cannot see them inside the keeper, but he knows his liberators intimately. Three deep, ocean-blue pills, the Dopamine, stamped with the name of the drug company, one blood-red pill (the Sinemet), and two of the Prolopa capsules, like tiny hourglasses marking the draining time he is to be granted among the mobile. "The quick and the dead," he used to say pre-Parkinson's, years ago standing between his parents in church. A child who believed the two were opposites.

"It's that thingy NASA sent into space, hon. You know...what's it called? You know, that thingy. Wait a minute ... they're saying. What are they saying? Hold on."

Myles can feel his hand beginning to calm, and with every nerve he can picture he wills himself, to the ends of his reluctant fingers, to pick up the pill box. He uses his left hand, the good one, to pry open the lid stamped with a "Tue" for Tuesday, while his right hand— still rolling its fingers as if taking bets whether or not he might accomplish his task—Myles holds against the top of the box for the simpler operation of leverage. Once the compartment is open, his right hand begins to calm and he is able to pour the pills into his right palm. This is the riskiest part, for Myles' right hand, despite the intense energy that he is investing in commanding it to stillness, might still decide to jerk and twist, rolling the tiny pills onto the linoleum and forever beyond his ability to pick them up again. He can feel the heat in his face from his effort, the sweat beginning to bead at his hairline.

"…or at least I think that's it. Galileo. Pictures from that space probe they're talking about. Omygodyoushouldseethis. It's sooo beautiful. It looks so smooth. Like a Christmas ball. With eeny-teeny pimples."

With one swift motion (no trembling!) Myles pushes the cornucopia of pills into his mouth. His tongue feels wrong—too flaccid. For a moment he visualizes his face, tightening his lips, willing himself not to let any of the precious medication fall out. He raises the glass Kate has poured for him at lunch and takes a swallow, washing down the pills. When he sets the quavering water back he feels a coolness spreading onto his shirt. It is slosh and spittle. He dabs at his face with his sleeve. His heart is pounding.

"Have you seen this, Myles? Never heard of it. My God, what we don't know!"

Myles is just thinking of standing up when he is surprised by Kate coming into the kitchen.

"Have you heard a word I said? I was talking about this planety thing they've discovered." She puts her hand on his shoulder. With the other she idly picks up the empty pill container and as casually puts it back. It is now beyond his easy reach. "They think it's got warm water oceans—just like ours! Under the ice."

As she begins describing the program, Kate's fingers very slowly move from his shoulder. Her voice is animated. Her hand, however, seems disinterested in science. It moves, inside his shirt, down his back, until she takes a chair. "So's I can sit beside you," she says. But the new vantage point allows her other hand to caress his chest, then move to his belly. Myles feels faint. Perhaps it's the meds. Not now, he wants to tell her, but he cannot breach the flow of words. She is describing volcanoes, crack lines across the ice that the probe, even thousands of miles away, can see. He will tell her. Perhaps later. Be careful. When conditions are better. Perhaps not. Her hand is, for all that, able to coax warmth from his legs. This can never go on, he tells himself.

"It's the smallest moon of Jupiter's, but still pretty big." Kate is saying to him. "Remember that spring in Edmonton we couldn't sleep for the river breaking up? Apparently it buckles just like that, only every day. Ice sheets miles high, thawing from the volcanoes underneath and the huge tides, shattering and freezing."

Myles feels his face flush. This is childish, this eagerness and hunger and heat and fear to speak. Kate doesn't stop talking. Her face doesn't change, even as her fingers become more assertive. Untying his belt (a practiced motion from preparing him for bed), she reaches beneath his underpants. Myles feels his chin become wet—in his distraction saliva has accumulated in his mouth. He swallows, coughs. She is not looking at him. But her hand is in constant, repetitive motion now, and his body reacts. Myles cannot breathe.

"Can you imagine the thunder?" Kate says. "The booming of all that ice breaking up?" Myles clamps his teeth. The planet shines, his eyes shimmer with blue and green, the rents of lava pour out.

Soon his pills are wearing off.

"They should be at the mall. Buying skirts." Kate's voice from the living room—is he imagining?—huskier now. "Imagine! Girls blowing themselves up!" It's five o'clock. The huskiness might be gin and tonic. In his good periods Myles has noticed the empty 26-ounce bottles in the garbage. Kate caught him rifling through the garbage, once, before he could teeter away. So far neither has said anything.

The sound of sirens from the television. Again the false, flat reporting of disaster. "It's crazy, this, what's happening. Don't you think? Why not make peace?"

"Peace is the last thing some people want," Myles says to himself. He has only minutes, now, to decide where to spend the next few hours as immobility sets in. Maybe he will go to the computer. The chair is comfortable. And he could find out more about this place, this *Europa*. Scientists think there could be life there, Kate said, in the warm oceans under the ice. What kind of life, he wonders? He thinks: Now that would be glorious. Alone and undiscovered, withstanding the mile-high tides rigidly locked mid-wave by such brutal cold. Then breaking free as the turning ball and volcanic heat bring the ice world crashing down. But alive; always turning, swimming, crawling, loving beneath the aching, frozen chaos. Still, somehow, alive.

About the Writers

Matthew Anderson is a parish pastor and a professor at Concordia University's Department of Theology. He lives and writes in Montreal. His work also appeared in the previous CBC/QWF anthology, *Telling Stories*.

John Brooke (www.aliette.com) is a writer/translator living in Montreal. John won the Journey Prize in 1999, and his novel *All Pure Souls* was shortlisted for the 2001 QWF Hugh MacLennan prize. His book *Last Days of Montreal* (Signature Editions) was published in 2003.

F. Colin Browne is a writer from Newfoundland currently living in Montreal. His projects for 2005 include a stage production entitled *The Benny Hinn Ministries* and a collection of short stories.

J.R. Carpenter (luckysoap.com) is a poet, fiction writer, and visual artist originally from rural Nova Scotia, now living in Montreal. Her short fiction has appeared in *Blood & Aphorisms*, *Postscript*, *Knight Literary Journal Volume II*, and the online journal *Nthposition.com*. She is currently working on a novel and A collection of short stories.

Jennifer Chew is originally from India. Her work has appeared in *Montreal Serai* and in *Shakti*, the publication of the South Asian Women's Community Centre in Montreal of which she is one of the founding members. "Loss/Survival" is a chapter from the novel she is completing.

Marguerite Deslauriers lives in Montreal and teaches ancient philosophy and feminist philosophy at McGill University.

Joni Dufour is a bicycle builder from Montreal. "First Light" is her first published work of fiction.

Liam Durcan lives and works in Montreal. His first collection of short fiction, *A Short Journey by Car*, was published by Esplanade Books/ Véhicule Press in autumn 2004.

Valerie Free has published poems in *Contemporary Verse 2*, *Pagitica*, and *Canadian Woman Studies*. In 2003, she was a finalist in *Bellingham Review*'s The 49th Parallel Poetry Award. She lives with her family in Montreal.

Carolena Gordon is a native Montrealer and great admirer of Italian shoes. She is a practicing attorney and is presently working on various short stories and a screenplay adaptation of "Shoe Salesman."

Alexandria Haber is a Montreal-based writer with several plays and award-winning radio dramas to her credit. Her work has been published in three other anthologies: *She Speaks* (Canada Playwrights Press), *Going It Alone* (Nuage Editions), and *Fruit of the Vine* (The Canadian Authors Association).

Carrie Haber is a writer, filmmaker, and rock musician from Montreal. Her latest project is *Pig Farm*, a documentary about an industrial pig farm occupying the site of a WWII Romany concentration camp in the Czech Republic. Her writings have been published in Canada, the United States, and the UK. Her music is available at delicaterecords.com.

Eyad Hamam immigrated to Canada in 2000 with his mother and sister. He has a degrees in microbiology and journalism but currently works as a freelance video editor for feature films and documentaries. He loves music, football (real football, the kind you play with your feet), reading, and animals.

Lynn Henderson is a retired broadcaster and the mother of four grown children. "How to Be" is her first publication.

Dawn Kackley is the author of a collection of short fiction entitled *Even This Is Love*. She has read at the Eden Mills Writers' Festival and in Toronto at Harbourfront. She lives in Montreal.

Ibi Kaslik is a writer, teacher, reviewer, and journalist. She is a graduate of Concordia's creative writing master's program and is a contributing editor for Montreal's *Matrix* magazine. Her debut novel, *Skinny* (HarperCollins Canada, May 2004), was well-received throughout Canada. She lives in Montreal.

As teacher, musician, actor, film editor, and parent, **Sidonie Kerr** has always been engaged in the telling of stories. After editing documentary films at the National Film Board of Canada for twenty years, she turned to writing short stories.

Michael Kosir moved to Montreal just over two years ago in a leap of faith. You can find him, year-round, riding his bicycle or laced into a pair of skates.

Neil Kroetsch is an actor, writer, and translator who lives in Montreal.

Brent Laughren is a writer who lives in Montreal. He is currently working on a novel set in rural Québec in the 1930s.

A former member of the Canadian Weightlifting Team, **Neale McDevitt** has published fiction in literary reviews and anthologies on both sides of the border. In 2003, his short story collection *One Day, Even Trevi Will Crumble* was named Best First Book by the Quebec Writers Federation.

J.D. McDonald was born in Toronto and educated at Glendon College, York University. He pursued graduate studies at the University of Sussex, the London School of Economics, and the Institute of Strategic Studies in the UK. He lives in Aylmer, Québec.

Rachel Mishari is an anagram. Another "Rachel Mishari" story appeared in the previous CBC/QWF anthology, *Telling Stories*.

Claudia Morrison is the author of a novel, *From The Foot of the Mountain* (shortlisted for the Hugh McClennan Award for English fiction in Québec); a collection of stories, *I Should Know*; and a collection of poems, *Arrival*, which won the 2000 League of Canadian Poets chapbook award. A retired professor, she lives in Pointe Claire with her husband.

Elise Moser's fiction has appeared in the anthologies *Witpunk* and *Island Dreams*, in *Broken Pencil*, and in the webzine *Lost Pages*; she has stories forthcoming in *Prairie Fire* and *Descant*. Her first published poem recently appeared in *Carte Blanche*, the literary review of the QWF. She lives in Montreal.

Maranda Moses graduated from the English Literature program at Concordia University in 2000. She is a Montreal-based writer whose byline has appeared in such publications as *The Montreal Gazette* and *Essence Magazine*. She is currently at work on her first novel.

Katharine O'Flynn lives in Montreal. Her stories have appeared recently in *Storyteller Magazine*, and her poetry in *Blueline* and *Bardsong*.

Deborah Ostrovsky grew up in Canada and studied history in Halifax and Toronto. She lived and worked in Poland during the late 1990s, travelling extensively in central Europe, the Baltic regions, and Iceland. Upon returning to Canada, she settled in Montreal with her husband.

Alice Petersen is a New Zealander living in Montreal. After graduating with a PhD in English Literature from Queen's University at Kingston, Ontario, she turned her mind to writing fiction. Alice's favourite Canadian occupation is shovelling new snow.

In 2003, at the age of 44, **Pierre W. Plante** graduated from Concordia University's English Department with a degree in Creative and Professional Writing. Pierre dedicates "Weathering the Storm"—his first publication—to his daughter Katherine.

Monique Riedel was born in Brussels, Belgium, and lived in a number of countries before moving to Montreal in 2000. She works as an agent, representing Canadian artists in the United States and Europe.

Connie Barnes Rose's work has been published in various literary magazines and anthologies, including the previous CBC/QWF volume, *Telling Stories*. She is the author of a collection of linked stories, *Getting Out of Town*, and is currently working on a novel.

Brett Schaenfield divides his time equally between the pursuit of literature, old vinyl, and good television. His sexuality is not up for discussion.

Kaarla Sundström is a sound poet who has frequented stages across the country and appeared in numerous spoken-word CD anthologies. She is currently teaching and editing and doing all those things word people do while pursuing an arty career.

Jeffrey Talajic studies English Literature at Concordia University. "Dumpster" is his first published work.

Barry Webster has published fiction and nonfiction in a variety of publications including *Event*, *Fiddlehead*, *Matrix*, *Prairie Fire*, *The Globe and Mail*, and *The Washington Post*. His work has been shortlisted for the National Magazine Award. He has just completed his first novel.

Alice Zorn has had short fiction published in various literary magazines, including *Grain*, *The New Quarterly*, *Prairie Fire*, and *Quality Women's Fiction*.

About the Editor

In addition to the first two volumes collecting the best stories from the QWF/CBC Short Story Competition, **Claude Lalumière** has also edited the anthologies *Island Dreams: Montreal Writers of the Fantastic*, *Open Space: New Canadian Fantastic Fiction*, and (in collaboration with Marty Halpern) *Witpunk*. With coeditor Elise Moser, he is currently preparing *Lust for Life: Wild Tales of Sex & Love*, due to be released by Véhicule Press in early 2006. He also edits the webzine *Lost Pages* (lostpages.net).

Claude's criticism and short fiction have appeared in numerous magazines, anthologies, and webzines in Canada, the United States, and the UK. He writes the "Fantastic Fiction" column for *The Montreal Gazette*.

His 2005 publications include stories in *The Mammoth Book of Best New Erotica 4*, *Tesseracts 9*, and *Red Scream #0*.

IN THE SAME SERIES

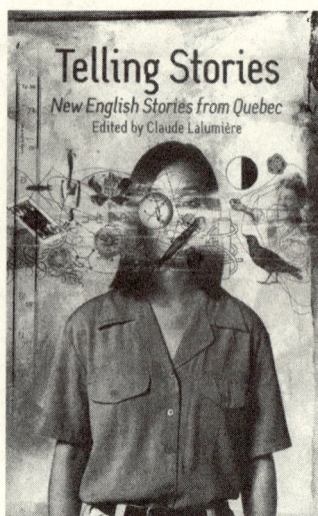

Telling Stories
EDITED BY CLAUDE LALUMIÈRE

ISBN: 1-55065-161-7

Véhicule Press
www.vehiculepress.com